COUCHSURFERS

NICOLAS BROHON

This story is about how travelling the world with no money, keeping your cool, dusting yourself off.

ISBN : 978-2-9555671-4-2

Couchsurfing is a new way of traveling. It means "surfing from couch to couch". The community members - the couchsurfers – meet up on a website.
Some offer free accommodation, others offer sightseeing tours, and others organize meetings. This network began in 2004 and has members in 200,000 cities.

Couchsurfing is free and it's a community in the tourism sector, just as Facebook and Skype are free communities in the communication sector. However, the fact that it's free is not the only attraction.

At first, many people wonder what the experience would be like. Indeed, the idea of hosting a tourist for free may be their worst nightmare; they may be scared about who they might be hosting.
You could be faced with thieves, or rude, disrespectful or bad-mannered people who might eat everything in your fridge and use your apartment as a free hostel with people coming and going at all hours.
However, there are many advantages, such as good company and the swapping of stories and you end up casting your fears aside.
You often find yourself wide-eyed with astonishment listening to a guest's stories over the kitchen counter, and these moments show that Couchsurfing is a concept based on rewarding encounters, heart-warming experiences, as well as saving money on accommodation.

Obviously, the rules that apply to you apply to the guest as well. There's no way around it.
Bear in mind that being a couchsurfer looking for an authentic experience makes a person adaptable, and being open-minded can make up for the occasional mistake due to cultural differences.
Unfortunately, a lot of people don't buy this argument. When they think of Couchsurfing they think "a stranger on my couch". Couchsurfing is not meant to simply host a stranger. We surely touch on a certain misconception.

This community can attract people with deviant behavior, just like any other community, but this is marginal.
Also, Couchsurfing has an effective way of combatting such behavior by providing a website where everybody can get to know each member.
This website makes it possible to track weird people down. This is the backbone. Couchsurfing encourages its members to report such incidents.

In 2012, Couchsurfing transformed itself into a start-up, going private and opening a corporate office in San Francisco alongside TaskRabbit, AirBnb and others in the prosperous sharing economy it hoped to join.

This book is about highlighting Couchsurfing.

1

Taking a flight out the hood.

The phone vibrates. A school needs a substitute immediately. Jérôme jumps in the car. When he arrives, the motorbikes are backfiring, the motorbikes are revving-up. At the entrance to the Psychological-Therapeutics Institute, sixteen-year-olds on the scooters they have pinched, are bragging like typical teenagers. Jérôme's eyes nervously scan the yard: no soul around. The gate is padlocked but Jérôme is running out of time. He has to climb over it although it is more than two meters high. The acrobatic movement is painful, the aftermath is tragic. There is a 20cm tear in his trousers. Damn, this slit looks big... Behind, young people are mocking. What can be done about it? The students inside are waiting for him. So he has to go anyway.

He heads to the office. The director is smocking nervously.
– Hi, sir...
The man stares at Jérôme blankly.
– Here you are. You've come a long way?
– 50km.
– Sorry for paging you so urgently. Our profesor felt faint after breakfast so he never came.
– No problem.
– Ok, funding run out. So, don't worry. Measured in terms of enrollment and drop out rates the situation has improved. But in this Institute, most of the boys suffer from an abyssal vacuity of their spirit. This is extremely common that they lose control of themselves. For example, the boys are very good at stealing personal keys. You can see in a minute. That doesn't mean endorsement. And we let them free-range although they consider themselves to be held captive...They are waiting for you in the prefab number one. Courage...
When he gets to his prefab, Jérôme puts his bag on the table. The scene is totally chaotic. The boys are scattered about the prefab. The swear words they are using reveal that they are gypsies. They are crawling through the closet, jostling and fighting each other, hustling for sneakers. They even

don't notice him. Jérôme is invisible to them.The younger the supply teacher, the greater the temptation to challenge him. It's not like the old hag who used to scream at us all day. And, despite his stern expression, Jérôme has little authority. Jérôme shouts out:

  – Good morning guys!
They turn around.

  – Sit down, please.

  – Why do that ?

  – We can start on this stuff...
So he reaches into his bag.

  – Mathematical equations.
At this moment, the door opens behind him. Diego, a puny 20-year-old student, with his helmet screwed onto his head, is walking past in company with a youth worker. His trousers are too wide and fall from folds into spirals. So, his legs look like corkscrews.

  – Be careful with him, he has been brutalized all through his childhood and was kicked out of the latest of a long line of colleges because of his furious outbursts. Last year he assaulted everybody he came across.
This is the kind of advice whispered to new teachers.
The young guy is standing still, facing Jérôme, and scowling. There is silence in the classroom. They gaze at each other, wondering who will blink first.

  – Sit down Diego, I've prepared some simple equations for you.
No reaction. The young guy is staring at him with an air of amused pity. Then he turns and looks round the room. He catches sight of a computer and goes towardsit slowly. Jérôme goes over to him.
The computer has already been turned on.

  – Can you turn it off and take a seat?
No reaction yet. Diego is looking at a scooter-sales website. Exasperated, Jérôme takes the mouse and shuts the connection down.
Furious, Diego pulls a cutter out of his pocket, stands up and cuts the cables behind the computer savagely.

  –Oh shit! Outrageous behaviour by some mindless idiots... sighs Jérôme, powerless.

Just then, a hammering starts rattling the window. Jérôme turns round anxiously. There are three adolescents from the neighbouring prefab, a fat one, a little one and a tall thin one, having great fun punching and kicking at the window that separates them from Diego, trying to break it.

– Oh shit...
Jérôme moves towards them, gesturing to them to leave but they have already got into the prefab. Meanwhile, Diego has pulled out a screwdriver and is trying to dismantle the alarm system.
– Are you crazy? Where did you find this screwdriver? It's not allowed! Aren't you strip-searched at the entrance?
There is a thud behind him and the zombies burst into the room. One of them grabs Jérôme's bag from the desk, rummages through it and finds a bunch of keys.
Jérôme runs towards him but the young guy has thrown the keys to his mate who is now racing towards the exit, kicking the door so hard he almost knocks it off its hinges, and storming out.
Diego, who is beginning to find this game interesting, stops what he was doing, grasps the hair of the one with the keys, throws him to the ground and grabs the keys.
The tall thin one escapes to his prefab from where his lethargic teacher, who has been slapped very many times, is looking on.
Diego speeds across the yard, chased by Jérôme. Then he gets into the building where three teachers, alerted by the alarm, join the chase.
After an exhausting high-speed chase, Diego is finally caught and brought to the director.

Jérôme is a stocky thirty-something guy. The main thing is he is fed up with his job. To tell the truth, he had gone into teaching on the spur of the moment.
Younger, he developed coping mechanisms trying to be cool, rebuilding in a general way after having been viewed as an alien, reading books around the clock as opposed to the non influent neighbourhoods he grew up in. He had been unemployed at the time and was looking for job security, taking the advice of those close to him.
One winter's day, he took the competitive exam for specialist teachers.

He was called in for the oral exam and his results were good enough for him to get through. Passing the exam was already stressful. But throwing himself into education was even more nerve-wracking, especially when they finally call you up for a mission. It was the first year that was difficult, and he suffered a lot of hardship. And they 've bossed him around enough. But he kept going.

He remembers sleeping in the cheapest and noisiest hostel in the town. That year was so hard he didn't manage to do any travelling.

From now on he would make the most of his free time to see the world.

2

Who rocks, who flops?

Jérôme turns on the computer. He logs in. A request appears in the mailbox. It is dated the day before.

Hello!
I'm Ana. I am a Colombian girl and I am travelling in Germany. I'm going to Strasbourg tomorrow. I'll arrive in Paris within 3 days and I'm looking for someone who has time enough to show me around some infamous districts. You do seem kind and I think that we have a lot of things in common. I speak French easily and I could teach you Spanish language. Are you free during the day?
See you soon I hope ^^.
Ana.

First, Jérôme hesitates. He had been browsing profiles for months now. But today it's time to accept. He calls out his sister Adele.
– Ok. Where's she going to sleep?
– In my room. I take the couch.

When he logs in later, another request appears in the mailbox.

Hello!
Actually I've just booked a ticket and the departure is for today. I arrive at 10.35pm.
See you!
Ana.

– Wow! Ana has sent a message at 1pm! She says her train arrives at 10.35pm, Jérôme trumpets to his sister.
– She was supposed to arrive tomorrow, no?
– My only option is to go as fast as I can and pick her up.

– Ay yo don't bust it out now. She feels bad, certainly, waiting for an answer.

– Get the room ready, please.

The train from Strasbourg is due in on time. Jérôme is losing his cool at the sight of so many different levels and escalators. He is under pressure. Could Ana have cancelled her trip? Finally the train comes into the platform. Impossible to distinguish a lost girl among so many similar outlines in the dark. The noisy crowd is making things very difficult. Jérôme looks at the photo of Ana. He's getting nervous as the platform empties when, suddenly, he thinks he recognizes her. She appears to be a pyramid-shaped girl. He's getting impatient. The crowd of passengers on the move is making him anxious. Now another unruly crowd is coming through and, that bounce right here, a girl carrying a suitcase. She has a cinnamon tan, a thin face, no cheekbones, almond eyes, a dazzling smile and dark braided hair cascading down her cheeks. Jérôme tries to visualise the photo in his mind's eye as he has no time to look at it.

–Ana?

She stares at him. He quivers.

– Jérôme? She answers with a sigh of relief. Thanks god! My trip was stressful. I was checking my mails around the clock! I was scared to sleep outside. And then here you are. Muchas gracias!

She hugs him.

–Yes, here I am.

–Fortunately. Sorry, I know it's short notice. I couldn't wait to come here! So I exchanged the tickets yesterday and I sent you a mail. I'm impulsive and emotional sometimes. I act too fast. But it's holidays and it's Paris ! She says smiling.

–You're lucky; I logged in by accident two hours ago. When I saw your message I hopped on the subway.

–You're so kind! Otherwise, I could have joined Couchsurfing local group tonight!

–Your suitcase is heavy, let me help you.

He drags the suitcase. They have to fight their way into the crowd.

–This is the adventure but I'm a girl, so I bring my entire wardrobe. Paris is the fashion town, isn't it?

–I live not that far from here.

–Ok, I need a ticket?

Ahead, a flock of humans hustles and jumps over the turnstiles.

–You don't, do the same!

–Hell no! I don't want to go to the custody for my first day!

–Ok, I bought one ticket for you. It will be easier. So, you have sent many requests?

–Actually, I've sent many but only three people accepted me.

–Why me?

–One of them was a guy with a big flat, but he seemed snobbish. The second was a young girl but she lived in the outskirts.

– My apartment is in the outskirts too, but very close. You could reach out Paris everyday. I live with my sister and his boyfriend Xavier, my best friend. We use to travel together.

– Ok, very nice!

– Hey, this is Ana, says Jérôme to the company.

Adele is sitting cross-legged on the couch. Xavier is sulking besides. Xavier is Jérôme's room-mate as well as his brother-in-law. His black hair is combed back. He has heavy eyebrows, and he wears the furrowed brow of an anxious man. He is over six feet two inches tall. The kind of guy that is running up credit-card debt to make it appear he had more money. He sits up and smiles when he sees the girl. What a fascinating and pleasurable pastime it has become for him to simply admire the feminine legs walking about each and every day.

– Welcome, engages Adele. You are a student?

– Yes, I'm studying architecture in Bogota. Every now and then I do volunteer work.

– Paris is a great city for you! There are so many different districts here! I'd have had you over to check it out but it's difficult with my schedule.

– Ok, what's your job?

– I'm an interior designer. I love it. The problem is that I don't have time to travel like you...

– I take the most now because I'm a student.

– You're right. Look at them, they're always complaining, these slackers. They are still away, on an endless vacation!

– Slackers? Speak for yourself! It's hard to bear pupils, says Xavier, before throwing cushion at her.

Ana is laughing.

– You are a teacher too?

– Exactly. I teach quantity measurement. But my pupils are business managers and they act like a bunch of angry young men.

Everybody laugh.

– Are they worse than Jérôme's pupils?

– He told you? Six months of happiness where I come into bloom at work!

– I thrive too! Adds Jérôme.

– That way you both flourish in your job, right? And you travel all together?

– I let them working it out on their own, says Adele.

– What are your trips?

– The Middle-East, Europe...

– You should go to Latin America! And you couchsurf everytime?

– Definitely on my bucket list. But last year I couldn't, states Jérôme.

– And what's your best memory?

– Iran, for sure. Xavier and I stayed in Tehran to a girl's flat. She lived with her cousins and her aunts. They organised a party for us. At night, they turned off the light, pushed over the tables and pulled us down the dancefloor. We were twenty. That was amazing! Far removed from stereotypes!

– Ana, is your first Couchsurfing experience? asks Adele.

– No, but I'm still figuring it out. I was so stressed! But now I feel good.

– Welcome.

– Thank you. I'm afraid, "being awkward". But I'm sure that my spirit change soon "Finally, we met !" Adele, you don't couchsurf?

– Only as a host, thanks to Jérôme. I cross the road of so many guys all year round. How bad is experience for women in Couchsurfing world? We hear about sexual harassment and the list goes on. Is there an unfair and swiping accusation or simply the inconvenient truth?

– There is no doubt that Couchsurfing is far from being a model of gender equality. But the root of the problem is the men think that it's a dating website.

– This is why I made the point in my discussion.

– Most people would agree that the state of the women is pretty bad right now but you gloss over the fact that it's a situation which is widespread in our society. Not in Couchsurfing in particular.

– I done paid taxes, paid dues, paid bills my whole life so basically I use Couchsurfing, simple maths, no numbers to crunch, jokes Jérôme. Ana, I show you where your room is.

– My room?

– Come on, you know the drill, you are our guest. I take the couch.

– You are so kind!

– It's weird, he is not so kind usually. No, I'm kidding you. It's an angel my brother!

He gives her an embarrassed look.

– I cleared some space in my closet. You'll get settled in. Make yourself at home.

– You can show me around Paris this week?

– It's a little complicated. But on Thursday, it's ok.

There's an opening at Galeries Lafayette. At the entrance, the artist is signing drawings for his fans. The line keeps getting longer on the stairs. *Phats & Small* has been turning heads. There is an exceptional view of the city.

– For your information, says Jérôme, the factories are located east because of the wind that sweeps the dust. Thus, the residential neighbourhoods are located west.

Behind, a woman stays stunned.

– I never thought about it that way... It's far-fetched.

They burst out laughing. They sit right next to an old man slouched like a field hand.

– We quickly get bored, he says. Gaze at this chick with ample bosom. Well, I have sledded down big ladies. She's mine, he spits.

Ana doesn't pay attention.

– Who can purchase that? Awful things! He splutters.

The old lady's already asleep.

– What do you think of his work Ana? asks Jérôme.

– Interesting job! I like Modern art!

Jérôme is locking into her lips.

– I'll get a drink, she says.

– Take two or three, says the old man.

– You help me? She smiles.

– With pleasure!

The old man twists with difficulty.

– I prefer to go alone.

Jérôme follows.

– Anyway, I would like to say thank you. You give me the day Jérôme. You didn't have to.

– You must be joking! I like spending time wih you Ana!

– By the way, I told you before that only a few people accepted me. That was not quite true...

– Really?

– I got a lot of messages from strange guys. These messages are often turned this way : « You're very pretty and you seem very nice ». Forget it! It's like to compare this to a dating site! This strikes me as a misconception.

– It's couch-dating! Have you heard this story about Riccardo. This Mexican guy noted that he lives in the "best neighborhood to go out and have drinks," that he offers a "cozy/clean/nice sofa/couch". He described himself as "amazing, outgoing, smart". Nowhere does the profile state explicitly that if you are an attractive female traveler, you might skip the couch entirely and wind up in Riccardo's bed, but it's a good possibility. In eight months using the service, Riccardo has let eight visitors crash at his apartment, of whom he's hooked up with five, for a 62 percent "success rate." If you count the additional two who climbed into bed with him for a cuddle and then fell asleep, the percentage climbs even higher.

– Exactly! These guys are using the back door! But this site tempts them into doing such things. They know what you like, what you hate, your passions, your job. Therefore, they know your mentality! I've even received a message from a guy who were flexing his muscles and who wrote « hey, I only accept girls ». Help! It's like : The more chicks I hosted, the better I am able to handpick those who want to have sex instead of those who merely want to use my place as a free motel for the night.

– That is clear!

– And I'm not being paranoid. I'm just going on a gut instinct. When I started, I was only browsing profils with references. Now, I'm a risk taker. I filter last connected profils. I'm looking very active profils. And among all these, I send a request to referenced profils and non-referenced profils. Surprises in store!

– I agree. A lot of couchsurfers behave like that because most of them are adventurers and they just not looking to get involved. They are kind of rebels and they use to break the common rules.

– Yes. So, what's the plan now? Eating an ice cream?

– Good idea!

9am, on Monday. Jérôme logs in.

Good morning.
I need help. I feel unsecure. It is my first day in Paris. Please, I need a host.
Jin-Sang.

Jérôme selects *maybe*. The same message appears on the community page of Paris. Jérôme is not enthusiastic because he has a lot of work. But he remembers all the positive experiences, the warm welcome he benefited from when he was abroad. He hesitates. It depends on his vibe and whether or not he wants to get involved. This girl could find another member of the community to host her.

3pm.

Hey, it's me again. I didn't find anyone yet. Nobody answers. Please, I'm looking for a reliable person for tonight. It's an emergency.
Jin-Sang.

Jérôme accepts. He arranges to meet her in front of the city hall of Malakoff at 7pm.

Behind her square fringe, her eyes scan the square panoramically. She has a round face and is carrying a backpack at least as heavy as she is. She seems stressed. Her features are drawn. The way she stands appears like a cry for help. She is afraid he may have cancelled, afraid of waiting in vain. The guy had taken a while before accepting her. Perhaps he has changed his mind. As she turns round, she spots Jérôme coming towards her with a friendly smile. She gives him a big smile in relief.

Jin sang stands still in the middle of the living room for a moment. She's still a bit checking up.
– Let me give you the tour, says Jérôme.
She listens to him attentively. It's been five minutes since she arrived but she is still carrying her shapeless mass. Xavier went on an internship and It´s a case of emergency so Jin-Sang will take his room for this night. Ana is going around, barefoot, flipping through a magazine and watching TV at the same time. She seems to be familiar with the place. This image relaxes Jin-Sang. It makes her feel peaceful. The corean girl possesses a near-perfect command of the English language what surprises Jérôme.
– That´s funny, says Ana. My first guest was a Corean girl. She was a little wary of me so she decided to sleep in her clothes on the ground !
Jin-Sang starts telling her story. The day before she left London to join Paris where she stayed with a couchsurfer. The guy was 60 and nudist. He was shamelessly strutting around her. But the worst part was that he didn't mention that he could just propose a single bed to share for the night. Needless to say, I left. She recalled the scene :

"He tightens his grip. She pushes him away, stabbing him with a stiletto and slipping out of the bed. She puts on her jacket, takes her bag and, in the confusion, she drops the sweater on the floor. She clears out in a hurry. In the streets, her skin is starting to vitrify in the cold. She walks very fast over the puddles, refusing to turn left or right, but going through the boulevard. Fortunately, several signs of stores and billboards illuminate at night. She goes into a Fast Food."

– I have fallen into his trap since the beginning. He offered me a place to crash during my one-night layover in London. He smiled in his photo, as if caught mid-laugh, raising his wine glass in a toast. His profile skimmed the basics: he had not posted a description of himself, or written anything in the category 'One amazing thing I've seen or done'. He picked me up at the station, I wasn't planning to. I didn't feel comfortable with that. He asked me for a drink. He paid it off. He followed me out all day long. Visiting the Museums... he either really gave a shit. As I walked away I thought, yeah, makes total sense. First he suggested me to another friend to host me later, outsourcing his perverted stunts.

Ana seethes with anger.

– It's a pattern of attacking women. I hope you gave him terrible reviews? Did you alert that there is a black sheep getting around? I've never in my life come across a guest like this again...

– No I didn't. I didn't linger on it long, I assure you. I dont feel anyway at all...

– Everyone kicks in, does their part. If you don't the risk is that it can happen to another girl. Think about all these ladies that have been through it. Raise awareness is a duty. It doesn't come from a vacuum! Do you think about that? Don't let people like him conceal their true face!

– She's right, advocates Jérôme. We both agree that you shouldn't let it go. Maybe this incident will encourage others to speak out.

– Come on girl, we're going to ruin his profile! There is nothing I would like more than to watch you beat the truth out of that animal, proposes Ana.

– With the greatest pleasure! I gonna bust it up!

Jin-Sang logs in and reads the entire profile of the old man. She clicks on "administrator report" in which she explains what happened. Then she skims through the references, she opens the drop-down menu and chooses "negative". She writes as an argument:

Go away from this predator. He sends you nice emails beforehand until you're trapped in. Indeed, you'll find just one single bed to share with. And if you agree you'll have the privilege to better know his wandering hands. A word to the wise... Run away!

– Here is, you can be at peace with yourself now because you did what you had to. That's the main thing, approves Ana. Now he is gonna be prohibited definitely. In California, I slept at a rich man home. His name was Samuel. He fitted out a room dedicated to Air B&B. There was a young Indian who rent. He was so uptight, always hidden behind the computer. And there was this scantily-clad woman, maybe she was 40 or something. She was a couchsurfer. She was so vulgar, walking through the house lightly dressed. In a word, it was disturbing the Indian guy. One morning, she was walking through with a bathrobe. She started to chat up everybody in her way. She was targeting Samuel in particular. Her panties were revealed to everybody's eyes! The Indian guy was occupying the best place. Poor guy! He was stuck on the screen! What is his opinion about the West?

She laughs. Jin-Sang gets impatient:

– How does the story end?

– She understood she couldn't go anywhere further with him. She got nervous bragging that any of her *Couchsurfing* experiences ended up in bed! She wasn't ashamed! After that she left the place and looked for someone else.

– After all, *Couchsurfing* is a microsociety. It's a mix blessing between trustworthy people and weird ones.

– My first couchsurfer was a Korean guy, starts Ana. He had been working for Samsung for 4 years. Those were his first days off. When I picked him up, he just had one day left in the place. Hard to figure out how he conceived his trip plan: one South American country a day. He was spending all his time in trains, day in, day out. When we got to my parents' place, I ask him: "so, what do you want to do now?". He said he wanted to see a sunset. I suggested we could join some cousins of mine outside at a famous café that was looking onto a nice view. He felt so excited that he started to dance and whirled. He couldn't control himself enough to stumble and tumble down the stairs. Poor guy...

– So what's about this sunset? asks Jérôme.

– The guy regained easily self-control. He wasn't going to spend his only Colombian day in hospital!

– He was a complete nutter! Jérôme notices. We have hosted five girls the week before. They were Danish. They worn us about their plan to cross Germany and the North of France by bicycle. We found it pretty cool. They were supposed to stay three days with us and arrive at noon. But even so they knocked the door at 10.30pm.

– Did they own a profile? asks Ana.

– That's the problem. Only one made the effort to create a profile. Moreover, when they arrived they were not really talkative. One in particular was out of humor. Then they took a shower on an assembly line, monopolizing the bathroom, reluctant to swallow the foods, and going to bed early. At dawn I have been woken up by the sound of bicycle bells. Looking through the window I could see them leaving out.

– Such daring! says Jin-Sang. Did you leave a reference?

– I regret not having done.

– You should have left a neutral reference, cuts off Ana. They didn't deserve a negative one because they were neither insulting to you nor insolent. On the other hand, a neutral reference could have spoiled their profile.

– It's disrespectful, adds Jérôme. The profile had nothing to do with the reality.

– It reminds me my background, says Jin-Sang.

3

Trippin out

Her eyes are blank, her eyelids drooping, and her mouth perfectly-drawn in crimson. She takes a breath of the cold air and tries to focus on something.

There is a ray of sunshine and she turns slightly. She looks vague. Adele takes a deep breath and closes her eyes.

Sitting on the residence steps, she puts out her cigarette with her index finger and readjusts her floral dress. She goes to the door, enters and closes the door behind her.

The sky is blanket of grey, the trees are bending in the wind and the streets of Malakoff are quite empty.

The pervading autumn mist rises from the ground and condenses on the windows.

Adele is lying on a cracked leather sofa, a pillow behind her neck, wearing a sky-blue pareo and giving Xavier, who is dressed rather more soberly than usual, the once over.

–You don't work today?

–Leave it alone.

–Your jacket is your working clothe, isn't it?

–I'm on leave till thursday.

–You're so sensitive for quite a while. You look grumpy and mildly tired. What's wrong with you?

–Don't pay attention. This job makes me crazy. Two years in a row. I need an escape.

–Really ?

–Your brother and I have planned a route.

–Really? I am not aware.

Adele strives to hide her frustration.

–Now you know. Next week we go to the Netherlands.

–I get a lot of work done. I take a break in two weeks, argues Adele.

–You can join us… He casually replies.

–I'm going to think about it.

A call is coming from next door. Adele takes the opportunity to leave this heavy atmosphere which is spreading progressively. Jérôme is running through his profil.

–It's Ana, she vouched for me.

–What's the meaning?

–It's a feature members used to indicate trust and connection to each other on profiles.

–What did you do to deserve this?

–I've been an available host. That's it!

–What is it about her that's so special?

–She was always smiling! Look, we are invited to Bogota!

–Cool. I guess the juice is worth the squeeze. This all makes me so motivated to create a profil and host people.

Loads of bicycles are piling up around the bike-park at the exit to the Amsterdam bus station. Xavier and Jérôme go on a coffee-shop crawl and in each one they take the legal-limit dose of cannabis. In the end, Xavier, who is saturated with this shit, becomes nervous. They gradually get lost beside the canal. They have to go right to the end of the canal path before they can find a way off it. They are at the end of their tether when come across Ann Frank's house.

– We've had enough, we turn like 5 miles loop. Ann, please, where is the avenue? I feel dizzy, so many canals. I'm seasick.

First, Xavier staggers. He stumbles and falls, exhausted. Then he crawls on all fours, holding his head, elbows on the ground, and bursts out laughing.

– All right, because I just want to get wrecked tonigh, all right ?

A swarm of giggly teenagers holding their handlebars high, proudly, go round them in circles non-stop. Jérôme helps his mate up from the dusty ground but he trips, slides and falls forward. Unaware of the situation, they look at the sky, which seems to be dropping on their heads. Xavier smiles. He's cheerful. He feels light. This town is so beautiful, The Amstel is so relaxing. He picks himself up. First he stays seated while unsuccessfully trying to use his left hand to stand up. He crawls along until he gets to a bench. The river is getting rough. The river is overflowing. The flood is coming. The waves are threatening. They should go. But where do they go from here? They are surrounded by the sea and trapped in a spider's web of a multitude of canals.

– I can see a bridge!

– Just take a breath so you don't black out on me!

Then it's the dark hole.

They can't figure out how they happened to be in a park. A hammer seems to be banging in Xavier's head. Jérôme stands up. He has now sobered up and is looking at the city map. Then he takes his phone and starts searching for the address of Joannes, who is to be their first host. It's hard to find. In fact, it is one of several student residence buildings far out of town and bordered by two parallel highways. After searching up and down the avenue they get to the residence, and look admiringly up at a huge complex. They look for building C. Van Gaal is on the interphone list. Jérôme rings and the door opens onto what looks like a car park - it certainly smells like one.Joannes is on the 3rd floor. Jérôme knocks and Joannes opens the door - he's a redhead.

– Welcome ! Come on in and meet my room-mates; they are relaxing in the living room.

They walk through a common corridor shared by all the students. The toilets form a big bloc which splits the floor into two parts. The flooded toilets remind those we use to see in the camping. The walls are covered with a lot of post-it. *"Flush and clean the toilets until the yellow tasks vanish!", or "use your towel and only yours!", "It is forbidden to flood", "clean your hairs otherwise you will clog the toilets", "take a daily shower is a duty ".* Between the toilets and the end of the corridor, several caddies are parked. Inside, mountains of litters run over.

–This is Berthold. He is a German. And this is Elisa. She's British. And Mylene is British too. It is my girl.

Mylene, who is of mixed-race, speaks to Jérôme.

–I don't know why but every time I go to Paris it is impossible to catch your French accent.

No reaction.

–And this is Anselme, says the orange feather duster. He is from Germany.

Anselme has a pale skin; straight blond hairs hide his eyes. The green
eyes enhance the pallor. Anselme is excessively fashion. His skin-tight
garment brings his excess weight to light with grace.

  –Do-You-Want-A-Beer?

Anselme articulates with so much exaggeration that he opens the mouse
like a fish stressing separately. It provokes mockery and giggles.

Mylene stares at Jérôme.

  –Tell me, how long have you couchsurfed?

  –Three years, why?

  –To be honest, in the last few years... ... our guests have dipped in quality.

  –What do you mean?

  –It's a totally consumerist approach to Couchsurfing that bother us. May
  be I can extend my journey one week, or something like that. Before it
  was a cultural exchange, and an exchange in many fields.

  –Yes, I met some couchsurfers that act and try all sorts of dodges just to
  avoid paying. Blame it on the TV shows that introduce Couchsurfing as a
  free accommodation.

  –This year, we've received so many profiteers!

  –Squatteurs you mean! cuts Anselme off. These guys send copy-paste
  without being able to write your name and leave like a thief , without
  saying goodbye!

  –We don't play that game.

  –This is why I accepted you guys, confesses Joannes. We identify high-
  risk profils.

  –Yep, if their profile are filled with mostly girls, cuts Elisa off.

  –I hosted a Corean girl when Xavier was out. She went through a bad
  time with her host who proposed a single bed to share. She stayed and
  that played out like expected.

  –What? says Berthold.

  –Either she got away from him and fled in streets. But she didn't want to
  leave a negative reference.

  –She was certainly afraid of having her fair share of insults. By the way, a
  negative reference will never stop a dirty mind to be hosted, continues
  Anselme. The guy could get along with another host who will thrill to
  his qualities.

–You heard the story of this couple in Lyon which hosted a Russian guy ? asks Mylene. They were planning to engage. The girl was unemployed so she took advantage of it to show him the town. And when his future fiancé left for business trip, she flew away with the Russian guy never to be seen again.

–Rectification, says Elisa, it is the fiancé who left for Russia!

–We are far, very far Couchsurfing spirit, concludes Mylene. With Elisa, we went in Germany to a couchsurfeur. We skyped with him before our coming. He seemed very nice at first sight. Thus we arrived at his home, he showed us where we were going to sleep. Each of us in a single bed, and him on the sofa. Up to there that was fine. The night comes, the guy was just driving around. There was something weird.Then he asked to Elisa "I can?". We pretended we did not understand. "We can just put the beds and sofa together" he proposed. But of course we refused and he laid down on the ground!

–It is not so surprising finally, assures Elisa. We shared intimate moments with our host, such as the rise, the bedtime, the evenings ...Automatically that strengtens the relationship. It is an unusual intimacy, that can either hamper you, or to create strong links.

Then he leads the French guys to their room where German people were supposed to stay before they cancelled. What a mess! There is a bunk bed and a mattress on the ground, a couch that needs some fixing. The carpet is soaked with food leftovers.

– We have a suggestion. Could we get a sneak peak on your Red Light District?

– Haha obviously everybody wants to see this place!

– Ok, let´s go. But first we take a shower!

The Red Light District is a place where the sex is king. Most of the visitors are French people who can easily reach this place by taking the Thalys. Behind the showcases decorated with red neon lights, the girls strut and reveal some parts of their meat to male public who is standing in a single-file and stepping on toes. The majority has his beady eye on it. What is funny is that the district is split ethnically. On one side, African and Latinos are cutting their nails, with legs apart, waiting for a man to bite.

Some of them stick out their tongue and rub their pussy, others take a look outside, tease and tantalize the few people passing ahead. On the other part of the district there are east girls on display shaking around and sticking to the window. One gets the look of a grim-looking secretary, glasses on her nose. The men arrive in droves. In a dead-end, a big guy takes the plunge and gets into a room. The fellows get excited, applauding and shouting cries of victory. The red curtain falls on.

However... here we have an awkward moment, when the time comes to wonder what should I do to honor my host? Should I invite him to the restaurant? Or should I offer him a gift?

– We invite you to the restaurant, Jérôme proposes to Joannes and Mylene. You can choose your favorite one.

Feeling caught off-guard, Xavier almost crushes in his fervor. The proposition does not fall upon deaf ears. The travel guide recommends the Keizersgracht as one of the most chic restaurants of Amsterdam. It's a restaurant that is highly rated. It's a reminiscent of a luxurious men's smocking club – hearty steaks are served alongside a wide selection of wines.

– I'd kinda like to try it!

– That's a surprise!

A sneak peek on the menu; the prices are in the order of 45 Euros and 70 Euros, the cocktails approach 15 Euros. Drooling, Joannes sets his sights on a menu which costs 67 Euros, including the filet mignon. To the great displeasure of Xavier whose the forehead becomes muggy. Mylene raises the stakes to reach 71 Euros.

– This stroll makes me thirsty, the slobbering redhead Dutchman points out. What would make you happy Mylene?

She hesitates.

– What a surprise, now the girl is thirsty, cringes Xavier.

– The Gin Fizz, she dares.

Staring at her, Xavier doesn't find any appeal; her flat nose barely hides a ghastly skin, the fat covers her body. Like a cavern, her mouse contains treasures so deeply buried that we couldn't catch the color: a stream of stupidities every time she opens the mouth. Her narrow eye seems to be staring him down.

– Damn unpretty, murmurs Xavier.

– What's your choice Jojo? asks the paunchy girl.

– Who is Jojo? asks Jérôme dishonestly.

– Jojo… Next time she calls him like that I'll knock her teeth in, whispers Xavier.

Joannes keeps on talking.

– I'm tempted to drink a Vodka Sling.

– And later what? We can expect them to gargle with an Absinthe? says Jérôme sarcastically.

After many delicacies, including horse meat and some snails, an average of height cocktails each one, the bill reaches 324 Euros. Xavier is overwhelmed, Jérôme is covered in sweat and goes to the latrines to mop his brow.

The sun is at its zenith. From the top of the walkway between the two platforms, the view is amazing. Framed by the Schiedam gate and the Rotterdam gate, the Schie River sleeps peacefully. Three and a half centuries have gone by but the painting by Johannes Vermeer sharing the authentic charm of his home town is still intact.
The main village square is teeming and the tower bell ringing. Chip and prawn-cracker stalls abound alongside the Gouda shops. Tasting sessions attract tourists as carrion attracts vultures. The aromas of fried foods wake up Jérôme's taste buds. He decides to do full justice to these foods by sitting down to eat them on a bench. He settles on the one free space he can find … until he spots an old lady standing beside him looking tired and he gives up his seat. The neighboring streets are empty and the Rembrandt galleries seem to be losing out to the delights of the food stalls and the sunshine. You can cross different bridges to go from one canal to another. In an alley, from behind a window, a Gypsy seems to be mocking the passers by. A windsock is indicating strong wind and Xavier suggests making tracks to the next host.

There's a smiling girl behind the counter. She has guessed who they are. She gives them the keys and tells them where the building is. It's in a quiet neighbourhood not far away. The architecture is typical of London and the people who live there are upper-middle class. Reddish-brown leaves make the sidewalks orange. When Jérôme and Xavier get into the building they are confronted with at least fifty stairs. The inside entrance is reminiscent of a doctor's surgery, or a lawyer's office. But the apartment itself is cosy with a high-quality solid oak floor, classy sofas and good quality hand-made leather armchairs. There are various pictures of the same old lady - probably the host's mother. In the spacious kitchen, there are a lot of spirits and hard liquors that Jérôme could not afford. A post-it informs the guests that they can eat or drink whatever they like. However, there is something else even more attractive : a desk in the office covered with mountains of coins and euro notes. There are stacks of 10 and 20 euro notes. Could there be a hidden camera on the closet? the French guys wonder.

In any event, no-one dares to touch a single coin. The bottle of wine is nothing compared to this display. Xavier slouches on the sofa. He is perplexed. He contemplates the pictures and wonders whether this Good Samaritan might   have witnessed some   sad   event in   the   past. Why should he want to share his comfortable life? Why does he blindly trust strangers? These strangers who will wash the dirt off their bodies in his shower, might spill drink on his luxurious carpet and soil the toilet or the tiled floor. Could he be seeking to atone for something or to repent for some past sin?

-It freaks me out. What does that mean? Why he let us in? Could you do the same to your guests? Displaying all your savings like this?

- I'm gonna make a selfie for Adele. The same scenario that Blair witch.

- You mean, you've got a piece of snot hanging out of your nostril?

- Yeah... "Adele, please, get us out of here. We are trapped with a strange guy hidden in the closet. The guy cracked a crib! He is planning to rip us off... Look, I'm scared..."

- You know the drill: mo money mo problems.

- Yeah, the more money we come across the more problems we see.

The following morning, Jérôme and Xavier are   expected at the Café Madeleine where a copious breakfast has been prepared. The waitress from the day before, as dazzling as usual, explains the menu and waits for them to react, as if she needs their approval: scrambled eggs on pancakes dipped in maple syrup and a salad, hot chocolate with cream. Jérôme and Xavier have a rather uneasy feeling about this situation. Tobias, their host has not yet arrived. He was supposed to be there at 8am. Another strange thing is that they are the only two clients.

-This is the most refined breakfast I've ever eaten in this miserable life, remarks Xavier gobbling up his eggs.

-I am deeply embarrassed. Do you think we ought to pay?

-No. This guy is generous. But this whole situation's fugazi.

After their breakfast it is time to go. Xavier wipes his mouth and goes out. Jérôme leaves a thank you note for the waitress. They are going to spend the next two days in the same area, with Tobias.

It's 8pm. The guys arrive at the triplex where Tobias is waiting for them. Tobias is 60 and has more than one thousand references, most of them as a host. **Jérôme is feeling awkward, a bit scared.**

-Don't panic bro. It's all arranged now. Be brave. Don't panic.

-But this time it's an old guy. We'll probably have nothing in common. Imagine the atmosphere. He certainly makes a good living.

-So you smile whenever he says anything and try to look interested, or frown. It's not really hard.

The old man looks rather dashing in a Brooks Brothers suit and Timberland boots. Bottles of Lowlands, Highlands and Speyside are piled up on the fridge. Tobias is not really talkative. He leads them to the 3rd floor, which is an attic turned into a guest room. The ceiling is not high. A woman aged between 30 and 40 is sitting cross-legged on a king-size bed. She stares at the strangers with her wide,round green eyes. She starts:

–   Hi. I'm Astrid.

That is a funny line! Xavier is sitting on a mattress on the floor and the person he is talking to is at the opposite side of the room. They are at least 8 meters apart and they both have to yell to hear each other. But the conversation is open and friendly, and makes them feel more comfortable in each other presence. After spewing out a few banalities, Xavier decides to sit on the sofa in the middle so as not to have to yell. Things start to get really serious, and then Jérôme's steps are heard. He says that Tobias has invited them to have a drink downstairs. On his way down the corkscrew stairs, Xavier, who is lagging behind, eyes the curves of the girl. Why arn't they walking up the stairs? What a shame ! The kid follows his look. Downstairs, Tobias is waiting for them by the fireplace. He is sitting on the red armchair. Two red couches are empty. Their vivid color and the fire create a warm atmosphere. Tobias serves from a bottle of Scotch whisky. Xavier and Astrid are sitting on the same couch facing Jérôme and the little kid. In the candlelight, Tobias starts a conversation by telling an anecdote about his experiences as a couchsurfer.

–In 2012, during the summertime, I was traveling across south of France. My plan was to visit nine towns and, to make the most of it, surfed nine couches. All of my hosts were single women between 45 and 60 years-old. The third one invited me at a restaurant and brought her A-game. She was making a pass at me. The following morning, I received a message on my phone. She was proposing me. She was giving me an ultimatum. She wrote that in case of rejection, she would kill herself.

–So creepy! comments Jérôme.

Astrid remains silent, holding her glass, sitting cross-legged. Xavier gives her a quick glance sideways. He loves the mystery women. Tobias ends with another story.

–It was during this year, when I hosted a Chinese student. At first glance she seemed nice. One hour later, someone knocked at the door. It was her five brothers begging for a room.

–Did you accept?

–What do you think?

As the evening goes by, Tobias moves and gets close to Astrid. But the girl is short with him.

–I plan to go to the Burning Man party this summer.

–What is this?

–It's an open-air party which takes place in the middle of the Nevada desert. People from all around the world gather over one week and form a self-reliant community. Would you like to join me?

Tobias waits but the girl doesn't react. He's a bit drunk and goes to bed. That means she's alone with Xavier now, and Xavier takes the opportunity to establish a closer relationship with her. He tries to slide his hand down her leg. Jérôme and the kid are playing chess. The girl must be feeling lonely, reasons Xavier, that must be why she's travelling with Couchsurfing. Maybe she's thinking of starting a new life, in which case, I'm the guy, he supposes. This self confidence that usually makes him stand out against challengers... Astrid doesn't move. Her refined, elegant lines, strikingly original profile and overall appearance make this girl unfathomable. He is seeking complicity but risks rejection as he looks steadily into her eyes. Her lips are firmly shut and it is as difficult to get any information from her as it would be to get access to the Vatican safe. In what he considers a tender gesture, he puts a finger on her ample bosom and tries to kiss her. Then he gets a slap he will never forget and gives him tinnitus. He should have been more cautious - his pride is severely wounded now. He feels as if he's had a cold shower. He thinks she regards him as just a teenager. Fortunately, Jérôme is occupied. Xavier stands up and rushes in shame to the stairs. Astrid throws him a glance. She remains frozen. How could she be expected to share a room with a guy like that? What is even more horrendous is that she is staying with someone she doesn't know. But she has no choice; she doesn't want to make a scene, and the kid is too tired to be moved. So she goes over to Jérôme and hugs him. She looks at him and whispers:

–You know what? Your friend is educated, but he is not smart.

Upstairs, Xavier feels his heartbeat and the blood running strongly in his horses.

Jérôme downs the stairs. On the ground level, Xavier is standing in the kitchen, apparently alone, dreaming may be.

– Where is Astrid, I didn't see her this morning.

– At the bakery.

Astrid opens the door slowly with the kid, smiling.

– Hey guys what's up? I bought some Turkish bread and typical Turkish stuff. Are you hungry?

– Thank you so much, says Jérôme.

– Ok have a seat to my table for tasting this delicious breakfast.

Xavier is fear of looking into her eyes. But the girl is comfortable. She blossoms among the brambles. Xavier regrets what he did. The girl is open-minded enough to forgive him despite the fact he breached her trust.

At this moment, an engine noise outside interrupts the conversation.

Jérôme looks at the window. A Chrysler Viper is stationed and Tobias with 3 teenagers get off.

– Hello guys, I bring you three couchsurfers.

The girl introduces the first and greets Jérôme with a firm hug.

– Hey, I'm Elena, nice to meet you.

Her smile makes him lose his mind and he could be stuck to her scented skin. But by catching the look of the tall redhead guy behind, he understands that nothing will be allowed.

– They are from Latvia.

– I'm Alberts, says the tall guy.

– I'm Macs, adds the small guy.

Astrid stands up.

–Come on guys, we can share the bread together.

Tobias seems happy to gather so many people. Elena questions:

– Did you have a bad experience as a host?

- A few but let me think... yeah, there was this young guy I hosted. He was Danish. He came just to see a concert in downtown. He put his bag on the room and rushed outside, then came back at 2am. He left at dawn. Everybody listen carefully.

– I remember this Australian guy. At the age of 18, he broke away from home for young offenders where he was handed down since he was 14, as he used to say. He was doing odd jobs, hanky-panky here and there thus far. One day, fed up with problems he decided to take a year off but, running out of money, he needed to survive and he handled to travel with only 1 euro a day, eating rice. So I quickly realized he got bad manners concerning foods, especially serving himself. Icing on the cake, he burst into the living room, totally enraged, holding in his trembling hand a faded pull-over with a hole in it. He was crazy with anger because the washing machine damaged his only pull-over! I tried to say 'take it easy'. You know what happens with this kind of guy who aims to be pampered from tip to toes by others. Anyway, after that I forced him to leave. I doubt he found someone else.

– Wow, what an incredible story.

– But can you reassure me... you don't have stuff to wash?

Everybody burst out laughing.

The evening comes fast. Tobias proposes to go for a drink.

– Guys, free drinks until 11pm! After you pay.

– We are all for it!

– Astrid, are you motivated?

– Sure!

Soccer fans from famous teams are thronging to the rustic bistrots and to the many taverns around the old market where the Kölsch is flowing abundantly. The pub is filling up. There are huge crowds trying to get tables. They manage to get one in the middle of the pub and the Latvians take their orders.

– So many people get nervous here, says Elena.

– They get used to occupy this table. But you guys, unfortunately they don't like your face lol.

Macs is slurping his beer at head-spinning speeds what amazes the rest of the group.

– Wow! Cool down boy, you'll have to assume!

– Don't worry, in our country we know how to survive during the winter.

– Really? Is your winter rough? asks Astrid.

– Quiet more than here.

– So guys, you don't have any reference, right?

– Actually, a friend of mine introduced me to the *Couchsurfing*. My first opinion was that living with a stranger was very constraining, you lose your freedom, etc...I didn't want to share all my time, to be indebted to someone for having hosted me, you know what I mean?

– I can understand but generally, you can deal with your host. Of course you got a schedule to keep, some hosts accept that you go home after midnight, some others don't tolerate. In the same way, some hosts trust you enough to give you the keys, some others don't let you stay alone in their flat and throw you out early in the morning during work days. But in general, the hosts don't expect anything from you.

– I agree but are we supposed to host them after?

– It's up to you to play the game or not. As far as I'm concerned, I'm comfortable with hosting people, I don't like so much to surf.

A dreadful client came out of the middle ages picking his nose stares at Macs. The drool is dripping down his chin shaped like buttock.

– What a disgusting man, squeezes Elena. Hopefully I'm surrounded by 5 guys. But damn he's creepy!

– Be quiet, miserable... Hushhh! I have my habits here, Tobias whispers, getting nervous in turn.

Suddenly, Macs looks at the time.

– Guys, It is supposed to be done in five minutes! I'm going to take another glass.

– Really guys? You're gonna be drunk! smiles Astrid.

Jérôme smiles too.

–Personally, I'm done!

Tobias, astonished, scrutinizes the 3 Latvians rushing towards the drink.

– I'm staggered... what the hell are they doing?

He expresses a deep disappointment staring at the tightrope walkers coming back; one got 4 cocktails, another got several shots meanwhile the girl is handling with orgasms drinks.

– We have peace now!

Elena has a bright idea – let's hide the glasses and bring them out at 11.01pm. Sweat is pouring down Tobias's brow. This everything-for-free lark is turning out to be quite a challenge ! But they are becoming hardened and seem to be taking a liking to the game. He looks at them sipping their margaritas, revelling in the drinking session, and thinks about how things have turned out : it seems to him that somehow Couchsurfing has changed them and turned them into selfish brutes. They would carry on in the same way - out for whatever they can get, taking everything for granted. Tobias can't bear it anymore. He feels as if he is surrounded by a pack of rabid dogs. Even the owner who is usually so friendly can't buy this argument. Stranded, Tobias lies.

– I don't get bored but I should go, I wake up early.

– Oh, you work on Sunday? asks Macs innocently.

– I give a hand to my brother-in-law actually. We have to fix the garage, Tobias improvises.

The guy whose the falsehood is bubbling up leaves quietly.

– You can stay but without any car It would be complicated especially with the quantities you are consuming.

– We'll manage by ourselves Tobias!

– Perfect! Good night!

– Are you sure you don't want to stay there a little longer? asks Astrid. You're gonna be searched guys!

He leaves the bar, head down, under the claws of his old buddies.

The next day, in the train that takes them to Eindhoven, there are those who have an easy conscience and those who don't. Three black men are backed up against the exit door. They wear a baggy sweat. Shit...the dark circles under their eyes are overdrawn and Jérôme wonders when guys like them sleep. Wow, their hoarse voice proove that they're barely 20, outraged. But the funniest part might be the way they communicate; their arm movements form such things as enlarged and concentric circles that sweep all of her perimeter. You can add the high decibel level that attacks the suffering ears of Xavier. They speak French. One of them turns to Jérôme and asks :
– You're French?
– Yeah, says Jérôme.
– Where are you from?
– We live in Malakoff.
– That's in what ? Country?
– In Dagestan, mumbles Xavier.
– Are you serious?
– No no, it's on the outskirts of Paris.
– Ah ok , I know because I have a cousin that lives in Pantin. I prefer France. Here, everywhere you see racists on the streets.
– What happened? asks Jérôme.
– Next week, they celebrate Zwarte Piet. People say 'This is for your negroes, they like blonds'. Blonds are going to paint their face in black and wear an Afro hairstyle.
– They're going further, cuts the other off. They're going to paint their big red lips. They go crazy mad.
– They're mocking us.
– Where are you from? asks Jérôme.
– We come from Ivory Cost, you know. We came here last year. I was living in Turin before. But I yearn to leave for England. Over there, they don't care about your origin. By the way, where are you going?
– We find nice people online. We crash there. And we save the accommodation. We save all our money except for transports, explains Xavier.
– Ah Yeah I know. i don't like this.

– Explain why?

– It's always the same wealthy white graduates that are pouring out all over the world with only 200 bocks in their pockets while the outcasts stand on the sidelines. You will never ever see a poor Congolese guy in his countryside hosting white rich people. This system always benefits the same people. We're a tight group, and the rich would do nothing but benefit over and over again.

– And you are basing this craziness on what?

– This is simply established by rich hosts from the North that lay down the rules since the beginning. They choose their guest according to their affinities... Ok, this guy is an engineer in Los Angeles, this girl is a press secreary and she works for a Newspaper in Buenos Aires. You see? These profils have hundred times more susceptibles to be hosted. Those profils are 120 proof, better than this Congolese... To be hosted by what-d'yer-call-him architect in Paris or top model in Washington.

– Well, it's not that extreme.

– And it's this same herd of rich travellers who has come to lodge with hosts from poor parts of the world for free just to save 10$, supposedly for the benefit of locals. These guys that advocate friendship among all people but only in New York or Paris. Even while at home they spend most of their time perfecting that pissy look on their face, never talking to the neighbour. Bullshit...

– Well, if that's the way you feel about it... By the way, as far as I'm concerned, we don't operate this way, moreover we are not that rich! We've recently hosted a student from Colombia. It's not really a rich country, isn't it?

– What was she studying? How did she afford the plane ticket?

– Ok, you've got a point. But Couchsurfing is a global phenomenon, no matter what you think. You just need an internet connection.

Düsseldorf is just like a ghost town with its empty streets. No dog poops in sight. On one side, people from Cologne, so genuine but also rude, those who are opened to Europe, and who attract party boys. On the other side, people from Düsseldorf, level-headed people who live the humble lifestyle and create wealth in the region. Haï has been waiting for them since noon. She sent a message to Jérôme but he didn't connect. So, when they arrive, she is not in a good mood. This newly refurbished property comprises of 3 bedrooms. Haï is cutting vegetables like a machine. Xavier and Jérôme stand straight, uneasy. Jérôme offers assistance but he receives a rebuff. At first, Haï is reproachful. Haï doesn't accept vague explanations. This intransigence is accentuated by her Viet accent.

– Mad plans, I had a lot happen to me in Couchsurfing. In the process, I became extremely wary of people I host. Last week, I hosted a young guy from Denmark. He came here to go to a concert. I've hardly talked to him. He hardly had time to put his stuff down and went out. He came back at night and left at the crack of dawn, with a face like thunder.

As the evening progresses, they all relax together. In the picture pops a an Australian teenager who 'escaped from the boarding school where he has been imprisoned'. He's throwing Haï a stink eye. He's wielding a sloppy gap pullover.

– Your shitty washing machine damaged my sweater! I just have one!

– Wow, take it easy, calm down, says Jérôme.

Haï seizes the sweater and observes it carefully. Jérôme gets in the way but Haï blocks him.

– It's not important, she says. It's Stanley, a couchsurfer, like you. He arrived two days ago.

– Who are you? asks Stanley.

– We are French. We stay here this night.

– I'm sorry. But believe me, I don't have that much clothing...

– No soucy, answers Jérôme. But you don't live here. Haï is very kind to wash your stuff.

– Yep... It took me forever to find someone.

Stanley slips away. Haï looks at him with sadness.

– He took last year off with a bunch of his friends. But now he hitchhikes alone in Europe. He tries to survive with only one euro in his pocket. Each day he swallows rice, nothing else. Sometimes I propose him to share my dinner.

– It really is audacious!

– I proposed to host him one week but these people don't speak 'Couchsurfing', you know.

– So you are from Vietnam? When did you arrived in Germany?

– I'm from Saigon. Then I lived in California where I studied. I shared my room with another girl, a very little room in fact. I never went out, to a party or stuff. But one day, I was in my room when my friend dragged me out for a student party. Ludwig invited me to dance. And we stayed together. At the end of the year, we moved out here to engage.

– Do you go back there sometimes?

– Sometimes. My sister lives there and I couchsurfed two years ago.

– You don't need, you have a sister.

– It's complicated. His husband is a former Viet Cong. And now she realizes she's wasted her entire life. She's a desperate housewife. Recently, we went to visit them with Ludwig. Believe me, we've been distraught by their cold greeting. Ludwig is like a French for them. Germany-France there's no difference! They even think that Ludwig was in Dien Bien Phu. They consider me as a boat people because I escaped communism. For all these reasons I don't like to go there. In Vietnam, When you go to the market, there are two prices : one for tourists, one for locals. They try to rip me off constantly but I'm not taking it. At the end I'm tired. I'm a stranger in my own land.

– Does Couchsurfing work there?

– It's a communist country. Make sure you ask approval before hosting someone.

– Do you work in Germany?

– Actually... No. I return to University next month to study Spanish language. I need to be doing something. I shut my brain off too much time! All day long I stay alone, waiting for my husband. But life is changing. We meet people, and we are interesting in... other things. You reach a certain age when you realize you have to focus on your personal life, you mind your own business. However, at the end, the only woman that really matters is the one whom you got children. But it's too late. The other women you meet later are a sometime thing, they're stuck back in the past because they had their own life, children, house... Man acts on his own.

Haï takes a deep breath.

– Speaking of which, Ludwig is the one I've been exchanging messages, no? asks Jérôme. Does he come today?

– Ludwig's got a business dinner in Düsseldorf.

Shortly before 00:00, Ludwig is welcomed by his barking dogs. Haï would just be sitting there with a vacant look, in a daze. Ludwig shows up and says hello to the guests. Everyone's looking at him with these fake smiles plastered over their face. Ludwig is leaning against the wall, looking down. Jérôme wants to break the silence. Once Ludwig withdraws, Haï apologizes and leave the kitchen.

4

You go boy!

Jérôme is lolling on the sofa sipping coladas while Xavier is sampling a grilled fish, listening Men's Health Live on his audio headset. On TV channel 2, during the famous show of Oprah, the red hair fancy Julianne Moore is gazing into the eyes of David Letterman. On CNN, Larry King is arbitrating a clumsy debate. On TV channel 4, it is a documentary already seen on *Al Jazeera* channel. On TV channel 5, Scarlett is gazing into the eyes of Jay-Leno. On channel 6, Janet is imitating is brother. Albertine, the neighbor, joined them. Physically, she's the ersatz of Angela Davis with an Afro look, messy hair like Don King, the mouth is colored like a poppy flower, the eyes very slightly prominent. She's vivacious, eccentric. She is crouching down here, painting a huge canvas representing a human body from the inside. She is painting the bones with the sharp side of some credit cards. The Olympic Games in Sotchi are finished. Kiev, the unfortunate, is trapped. Euronews shows the civil war. Albertine analyzes, speaking with a sensual voice:

–It feels like being in Tchetchenie. The tyrant will destroy himself. Shakespeare...

Xavier, the mouth full, spitting on her face, retorts:

– And the whimsical Albertine spoke. You crack me up! Jérôme, how you can grant this girl access to our flat?

–The difference between me and you is that I studied. What about you and your academic failure?

Jérôme intervenes.

–Let it down.

A long silence breaks the friendliness. Then Albertine comments:

– Poutine got the Crimea as Hitler got the Sudetenland. Call it what you want, the Americans can show off, we see who really has the balls.

– Albertine, the poet...

– That is true. Take the Europeans. They draw the wood sword. They can do nothing to stop that. The guy wants his Empire.

Xavier is appalled.

–You speak too much but what do you do except making grand speeches? If the angels come down, please take her.

Albertine looks up.

- Acting. Yeah, I want to act. I am a pragmatic person. I plan to step up and head to Liberia in order to organize a coup d'état. I've been cut off at the roots. My battle will consist in ending the natural resource curse in the region.

- First, you had better ending drinking brandy. You're stuck on the Welfare system...What do you do besides babble for hours on end? Kind of rebel without a cause.

- Shut up and look at my canvas. I got it all! My pockets got fatter!

Jérôme sighs, raising the eyebrows:

- Here we are! The verbal fight begins. Please, time out! Each one keeps to its own side. End of the first round. And Albertine, ain't no need in being greedy.

- Your canvas? Are you mocking? It's nothing but a poor imitation of Basquiat! You create nothing. Black authenticity... one more undergraduate skull and bones activist...

- Shithead...hard to emulate...

Albertine is drinking a pint of rhum.

–Look. You can't even see straight. And stop smoking. You'll get something bad.

–But if we cut her tongue may be she'll stop blathering, dares Jérôme.

Albertine grimaces at them, face bruh...

- Fuck you, scrub.

- Albertine, why do you say that you are uprooted?

- Every hoodrat there gets to be a baby mama for some baller, except me. No it's a joke. My father was a farmer in Liberia. One day, a smaller one, a nomadic, grazed his cattle on his field because the pastures were better. My father was afraid to see his field reducing. So he threatened him with a machete but the poor farmer was carrying a weapon likened to a Kalashnikov. Guess the end... At this moment I left my country.

Adele appears with a cup of tea. Seated beside Xavier, she admires the canvas. Albertine looks at her.

- You know, every time I cross your man he jumps up at me. He's hungry, believe me.

– What are you talking about? He is not hungry, he has me.

– You are so naïve. What did he tell you about *Couchsurfing*? Dig into it. Finger tips on the hips...

Xavier agrees:

– Out of sight, out of mind...

– What's the hell! Are you confessing?

– I give it up to God! Come on, quit trippin'. Unfounded accusations...

– Doesn't take a genius to see...You let him free-range everyday...Trust me Adele. I'll be there next time and I'll keep a watchful eye on him around the clock.

– Sorry but I get myself in a tangle... I would like to know your conception about *Couchsurfing* Jérôme. You come with him so you know his state of mind.

– It's a sterile discussion.

– Hey dude, you're oozing. We hear about a lot of hanky-panky going on here, mocks Albertine.

– Keep on painting your horrors and keep your counsel! orders the presumed guilty.

– He's right, mind your own business. Mind your body rub parlour! adds Adele, typing on her laptop.

– Sorry, I speak my mind. You got shit for brains, you're so weak... But control your hoes, you let them talk to crazy! Hey Xavier, you'd better watch your back before she turns into a killer. Best for you and the situation not to call the beaner.

– Oh my god....your breath! You could wipe out a herd of buffaloes!

– Shit, give me a biscuit...

– Me too, you crack me up Albertine! says Adele.

– Not a fan of the gloating so...

Then Albertine starts singing:

– Honey came in and she caught me red-handed creeping with the girl next door. Picture this, we were both butt-naked banging on the bathroom floor.

– Shut up Albertine! It's like watching a chicken cluck!

– To be a true player Xavier, you have to know how to play.

Suddenly, Adele hyperventilates.

– What the hell is going on! She shouts. Up to 35 requests coming from Indian guys! In one week!

– Too much guys who lack a bit of women.

Listen: *If you open your door I open my heart.*

– Yeah, that's right!

– 9000 km far from there the risk is low...

– Get this :

> *I'm a cook. I could cook you something. I've got a peculiar feeling somehow... that sooner than you think, we are going to have a good time together.*

– How dare he laugh at you...

– Two questions cross my mind, guys :

> 1- There are no peanuts in Indian cooking?
>
> 2- Is that the way you send a request on Couchsurfing?

– Ah ah ! It's a bunch of Serial daters ! Well, I'm off to cement my future. Have a good night!

Jérôme takes Albertine to the door. Adele takes the opportunity to seize the hands of Xavier and stare his eyes.

- What do you do there? Tell me and let it off your chest.

Xavier observes her. He realizes how much she's beautiful.

–Nothing that can hurt you.

These words sound as a confession. Adele closes the eyes for a time. She takes a deep breath. She can't endorse it. Xavier freezes momentarily. Jérôme, stands behind the wall of his room feeling knots in the stomach. He lays on the bed and stares at the ceiling, overwhelmed by a guilty feeling. This night he will toss and turn for over an hour, unable to sleep.

5

Manhood.

At the end of the 80's, the multiplication of the images is favored by the creation of private channels undergoing the pressure of audience. The emotion takes over the analysis, the feelings over the reflexion. The images of the concentration camps in Bosnia broadcasted in TV were questioning the values defended by people from the west. We can observe the major consequence of this visual trauma in the representations that remain twenty long years later.
  – What? Are you seriously going to get there? But there is the war over there! Do you want to get wiped out?
  – Don't worry, take it easy. Before going to the barbarians, I am trying to get used with the wilds.
Brainwashed folks...

Jérôme logs in *Couchsurfing* website. He heads to Mostar page. He filters the profiles. First, the recent online members appear. He checks all the profiles rapidly. Almost every member mentions "prefered gender female".
  – Funny...
  – Let's face it. Guys like you and me don't have any chance.
The second page introduces some various profiles. One profile draws his attention. The girl is Dzana. She looks like friendly. She has 45 positive references including 7 as a host.

Hi Dzana, we are 2 friends who travel all over the world. We use Couchsurfing because it is the best way to deeply know the culture of a country. As far as I'm concerned, I do like to meet people, discover their way of living, their languages. And I love to cook! I'd like to meet you because your profile and the references left make me believe that you like to host people and let them discover your world. May be we could exchange about our respective cultures and you would show us around the unusual places of Mostar!
Cheers,

Jérôme.

In the mailbox, nothing new : 2 *accepted*, 3 *may be* and 6 *declined*. He checks on last time that his Croatian host hasn't change his mind. Everything is fine. He confirms him his arrival tomorrow at the end of afternoon. Outside, the weather is hot. Jérôme watches through the window. On this July 6th, Malakoff seems empty. The noise of the keys turning in the lock makes him losing his thoughts. A guy wearing a cardigan covering a chaste with large shoulders shows up. This is Xavier. Today, he is at least as excited as Jérôme thinking about discovering this part of the world which makes him think about war. They both were ten when TV was showing images of Sarajevo on fire. Those Serbian snipers stand on the roofs were targeting Bosnian civilians getting out in the streets when they were going to get livelihood. In the last couple of years in primary school, the name of Slobodan Milosevic was familiar to them. It happened for them to discuss in the corridor before coming in the classroom. Even if they didn't understand the objectives, they knew that some atrocities were committed in the eastern countries. Then, this new fellow with a name that sounds Yougoslav was participating to wake the curiosity of the two boys up. Now, they were 30 and they would have their own idea about this conflict.

– So, no bad plan? Everything's right? asks Xavier, carrying a lemonade.

– Everything's OK. I got it all planned out. Tomorrow, Zlatko will be picking us up in Split downtown. Then, on Sunday, we have an appointment in Mostar with Dzana. She just accepted our request. She looks really cool.

– Has she got some references?

– Yes, and quite a lot.

– She won't play a trick to us! Let me check it out. A typical couchsurfer stays on average between 1-3 days. This chick is spending a week or more at some guy's place, you can bet she's not spending those days exploring museums and art galleries.

– You imply...

– This is one of the obvious ones. Her profile shows that she has lots of male friends compared to female friends, that's a strong sign she prefers to be hosted by men. Take a guess why.

– Are you serious?

– Furthermore, the closer she's to her "male friends" as shown by "relationship type", the greater the chance she's way, way more than just friends. An easy way to see which "friends" got her beak wet is to look for strong relationship types such as "best friend" or "close friend."

– You are on sick cat, you know that?

– Her profile is filled with mostly guys from exotic locales such as Brazil, Jamaica, Italy, and an assortment of Latin countries, then you can bet she's not doing for humanitarian reasons. Finnish girls only travel for sex, especially to Latin America. But we're on holidays, so let's have a fucking good time!

– What do you mean by 'fucking good time'? asks Adele after catching the conversation.

– Hey girl, why you sweating me?, I have no idea what are you talking about?

– Great, Xavier, I'm glad you think I'm a complete idiot.

Xavier steps forward and wraps her. Adele is so fragile compared with him. She looks like a Spanish girl with her dark and curly hair, and her brown skin.

– If you want, you can come with us?

– You know that I don't have as many days off as you.

– Next time?

They kiss. Adele pushes Xavier on the sofa. She gets on him and smiles. She puts her chignon off. Embarrassed, Jérôme leaves the room.

The radio on the bus is playing the local crooner, a melancholic voice on a loop. Six chords repeated incessantly. On this summer evening, the Dalmatian coast, more rocky than sandy, suddenly gets very windy, and the calm Adriatic Sea looks breath-taking. Dusk comes down as they approach the city. The twilight bathes the stone villas in a golden light. The two travellers can soon see Split, the pearl of the Adriatic. The journey had been long and gruelling. Eleven hours on a bus with on-board toilets so tiny they had to pee in the female position. On arrival in the city, the Polish driver orders everybody off. The passengers retrieve their luggage. Jérôme and Xavier have only a backpack and are hoping their host will do their laundry for them. As they get off, they are assailed by a crowd of old ladies pushing and shoving each other aside. Each one is holding up a sign bearing the word «zimmer» - they are offering small rooms to rent for a pittance.

It could have seduced them; they would have the impression to contribute to the economy of the country. All the more since Croatia just joined the European Union. But it is not the main reason. These old ladies don't speak their language. And they stammer only a few English words. Above all, the visit of the town and the conversation are not included into the price.

Never mind, the two fellows rush to the downtown. They cross a number of narrow streets. They contemplate the ruins and cross several ages at the same time. A real superimposing of historical periods, from the column of the Egyptian Sphinx to the shadow of the Shrine transformed in temple. We slide on the pavement in glossy limestone. The center is constructed in the middle of the rest of the Emperor Dioclétien Palace. The granite and marble columns erect. Under the archway, the old ladies take their dried linen back. Jérôme and Xavier climb the stairs of the bell tower of the Cathedral. Finally, they arrive in Narodni Trg Square. The square is surrounded by ancient houses. In the Trg Republike Square we can recognize the residential building of Zlatko owing to the ogive windows. Xavier is suddenly suffering from a stomachache.

– It bothers me a bit. It's late, we're gonna disturb.

– Do you think so? He must be used...

– *Couchsurfing* is fine but we must be daring. Each day is a new challenge. Eventually, you don't know if everything will be OK. And if we don't get along with him, it could be long.

– Stop thinking like that, I am having doubts now.

Xavier opens the main door easily. He crosses the backyard with a bit of gravel, followed by Jérôme. No noise, only the sound of the sea which is located a few meters far from the house. A stone staircase leads to a door in solid oak. There is no bell but a knocker in metal.

– What do we do?

At this moment, Xavier would swap his invitation for a bed and breakfast. Jérôme knocks the door...

– We are not going to stand here.

– What are we supposed to say? It would surprise me if he is smiling at this time. Maybe we exaggerate…
– You red his profile as I did. He looks really cool.
– You're right. I think I'm misreading.
While knocking, Xavier realizes that the door is open. Jérôme puts his belonging on the sofa while Xavier reads the message hanged on the wall.

Xavier and Jérôme,
I am sleeping but feel at home. The room located upstairs is empty and you can use it as you want. I left some blankets on each bed but if you're cold, you can take some others in the wardrobes. If you need anything, don't hesitate to wake me up. I can provide everything you need. I hope that your bus trip was safe and that our home was easy to find.
Have a good night and see you tomorrow morning.
PS : If you wake up early, you can take some milk and jam in the fridge and some biscuits in the right cupboard.
Zlatko.

A young thin man wearing a green-striped and with a snub nose knocks the room door. He shyly shakes the hands of the friends and invites them to join the living room. Downstairs, a girl finishes her breakfast. Her baby face contrasts perfectly with the emaciated face of Zlatko. She wears a mustard-yellow tank top and a tight jean. At first sight, this girl looks shy. However, she doesn't hesitate to start conversation. What impresses first the French is the perfect command of English that weirdly have a good number of young Europeans. She introduces herself as Blanka, Zlatko's roommate.
– What attracted you here?
Obviously, this is not the real question because the answer is so obvious. But it allows to carry on a more troubling question.
– What image of ex Yugoslavia do the French have?
Jérôme hesitates so he settles for vague replies.
– The French people are not so much interested about this part of Europe, he pretends awkwardly.
Then, he puts things right claiming that Sarajevo and Kosovo stick in people's mind in the 90's. Blanka smiles and gives Zlatko a friendly

glance. Definitely, the tourists don't understand anything about this country.

– I'm going to tell you my unique *Couchsurfing* experience. It was in Munich three years ago. My host was a twenty years old girl who was making confusion between Croatia and Bosnia. She had preconceived ideas such as I grew up in the civil war and persecution. She all had matters to introduce me to the civilization world, the German decency, the parties in the pubs, the gathering of young people in the parks. Anyway, all these things that I didn't get the opportunity to experience during my horrible youth. I ended up acting the part of Cosette. So I have benefited from the best Third Reich museums in order to realize that Germany had certainly lived a worse tragedy than Bosnia. My country wasn't so unfortunate compared with Germany. I had crawled to the best pubs and drunk the most delicious beers of Munich. On top of that, even if Zagreb was not Sarajevo, it had been shelled too. So no, I didn't steal my favors!

Zlatko was born from a Croatian mother and a Serbian father. But at home, they never talked about this topic. War was over. He was raised in Krajina, this Croatian region near the western border of Serbian Bosnia.

– I dream about living in Western Europe, he confesses. One day, I will settle there definitely. It's this future that I hold on to. Anyway, the integration of Croatia in European Union doesn't give some real outlook for young people. We are too far from the big European cities.

Blanka has to stop herself from smiling when she hears him talking about his country very negatively.

– Anyway, you shut the doors yourself by choosing psychology! For us, the war is far, so we are not traumatized anymore. Oh, it's not like you were any help!

They all start to laugh. Then, it's Zlatko's turn to question the French.

– Is it true that in France, there were collaborators of Nazis like in Croatia? They were a lot in Zlatko's region.

– They were a lot, Jérôme answers, but if I had lived during this period, I would have fought them with all my forces!

– For sure, claims Blanka.

Suddenly, a kind of new hippy shows up. This figure is skinny, all his members seem to be stretched. His hooky nose plus eyes like sharpshooters make him mysterious.

– Here comes the dreadlock science-geek Aleksa.

It's difficult to imagine how this shock of hair doesn't provoke him a stiff neck.

– Hey guys, wazup? I come from Belgrade. You are from Belgium, right?

– We're French actually.

– Say it again?

– France.

– Oh sorry actually we are expecting Belgium guys next week...

– After months spent hosting so many people, you cross paths with strange ones, confesses Blanka. As recently as last week, we've hosted a couchsurfer. He said he thought that the food was ordinary. When he asked me for other foods, I just got blindsided!

– Occasionally, there are unexpected situations, says Zlatko. Some guys arrange a date for coming but they don't come. It reminds me this couple from Malaysia. They announced a date but they arrived, like, a week late. They gave us the excuse that we didn't speak the same English language! Aleksa sits on the ground.

– To be honest, it's a bit confusing sometimes because you can cross a different couchsurfer each day passing through the living room, another appearing just because a couchsurfer opened the door. Most of the time Zlatko and Blanka forget who is supposed to come.

– Very squarely, it depends on the relationship we established before. For example if we stay tuned by *whatsApp* and we get along very well I come to pick you up at the airport. Otherwise, the door is always open but not sure that we hang out together, right? Because *Couchsurfing* is not a free accommodation. It's about a long-term relationship. I host you now, you'll host me later.

– A terrace in downtown sounds good for you guys? says Blanka.

– Why not!

The Irish pub is full of Europeans, the deafening techno-music stops people from speaking. Xavier starts a conversation with Blanka whereas Jérôme gets closer to two Berlin girls.

– One's company, two's a crowd, Xavier proposes grabbing her by the hand.

Zlatko follows them but Xavier anticipates and gives him a wink.

– I'm going to go get a drink, says Zlatko.

Outside, the music plays loud yet. Xavier stands against a car triggering the alarm.

– Fuck, ever hear of the word privacy?

He lits a cigarette and inhales deeply, staring at Blanka. Then he laughs.

– What is funny? Are you drunk?

– Are you squinting when you drink? It's so charming!

– Don't take me for a fool! You are acting kind of shady. I rather gentlemen...do you have a girl in France?

– We broke up recently. She's effin' with my effin' head. You know what I mean, feeling bored. (He takes a sweet female voice, setting burst of laughers). Where have you been? Let me guess...hanging out with your gang? I don't like them, they stick, they yell, they smoke. Pffff gossip! It was driving me nuts at the end!

Xavier blows the smoke out and scrutinizes her. Instantly, he gives her a hint of a smile. They cuddle so strongly that they stumble over a group of three guys. One of them hits back at Xavier straight after and pushes him back. The latter jumps on the assailant. He heads-butt him so that the offender falls buttocks-first on the pavement. Then he throws his hands around his neck. Blanka intervenes.

– Calm down Xavier!

At this time, the two guys behind take the opportunity to kick the chest of Xavier who stands up quickly and punches the face of the nearest guy. This one staggers until hitting the ground, getting his bell rung, looking around for Xavier. As proud as a peacock, the destitute starts fighting again, trying to bounce back while Xavier turns back and faces up. The disjointed puppet is totally out of control. He flails weakly but the punch he receives on his face makes him knocks out.

– Stop Xavier! Come on, we get back inside!

– He blew his frickin' face off!

Around, everybody is watching without flinching. Xavier, feeling a rush of adrenaline, grabs her wrist, heading her to the dance floor where the loud music turns the dancers on. Zlatko and Jérôme join them. They all are spinning around under the lighting effects and Xavier takes his top off what is setting off a burst of laughers. Xavier picks Blanka up off the ground spinning together around with gathering speed. Their friends go hog-wild, yelling, jumping, crowding.

It's been over an hour and people are still waiting on the platform. Anyway, there is only one train to Mostar. No screen, no information, no announcement. No worker either. Only some tourists are getting impatient. On the facing track, a desperate mother with his son is strolling around, begging. The kid is blind, the skin growing yellow by the dirt. Poor kid. Nobody cares. Crossing the railway tracks would be forbidden if we were in France, but here there is no gateway. Anyway, there is only one train today.

The train arrives. The interior is outdated, damaged. The discomfort is worse than the French trains during peak hours. Sadness makes the elderly surly. Outside, the landscape is wonderful; the green mountains overhang the blue river. Jérôme and Xavier contort themselves to slide their ID in the shoes. Here is the plan: they don't speak English, nor French, neither Spanish. At best, they stammer back slang. A little girl sees the hand of Jérôme sliding a wallet in his underwear. She stares wide-eyes and whispers some words to her mother who glares at him. At the other side, the control officer is punching the tickets. She rushes towards their car so they have to move quickly. Hopefully the next stop is close whereas the officer is just 5 meters far. Xavier overtakes an old lady who is controlled. Fortunately, the old lady is awkward so she takes time to find her ticket and Xavier takes the advantage to turn his back while the officer is making an announcement. The door opens and the guys get off the train, rush towards the other side and embark hurriedly. The train starts again whereas the French people are drawing attention to themselves. The officer comes back, sticking her nose over the horizon. Xavier is leaning back against the fold-up seat as the officer heads for the first class. No more time to lose, Jérôme walks fast at the head end of the train, pushing two or three passengers, then looks back at the officer hurtling up at top speed, indefatigable, as if her brain is conditioned to select those who are within the law and those who aren't. But even so it's too late, the platform already appears and the guys disembark.

The old city of Mostar is nestled in the deep valley of Neretva. The numerous Turkish houses in the Old bridge area Stari Most have both ottoman and Mediterranean features such as multiple copulas, pencil-shaped minarets. Jérôme and Xavier are walking along the famous bridge on the Muslim side looking at the store keepers selling bracelets, porcelain factories, paintings. On the bridge, a young guy is waiting for the crowd to dive into the river. Further, they reach the town of Mostar and join a villa which is facing the bus station. Dzana is a 33 years old dark lady. She lives with her old sick father in this duplex where she occupies the first floor and lets the ground level for the guests. She offers coffee and starts conversation.

– I use to travel by *Couchsurfing*. Three years ago, my ex and I went to Indonesia and it was our first experience as surfers. Arrived on the doorstep of our family host, the father changed his
mind and turned us away when he realized that we weren't engaged with my boyfriend. After that we sent a request on *Last minute Couch Request* and another host welcomed us in the outskirts. I know what a host ought to be; I mean good manners.

Xavier is absorbed with her, she looks so smart.

– Tell us about your life here.

– I work as a teacher in the public middle school in which Bosnians and Croatians are separated. The pattern of variable working times within the school works well.

– Are we on the verge of something potentially cataclysmic? Outside, do they talk each other?

– Obviously. The situation is tricky but not impossible. After school nobody control what happens even so some families are reluctant. The government lays down the rules but what I mean is that nobody can compel someone to love someone, as long as you abide by rules, no problem. But against all odds, the new generation is changing the mindset even if it's a bold gamble. Most of the students were born after the war. Bitterness is gone! Up to now, we avoided a cataclysmic scenario; indeed, so many Bosnians hit on Croatians girls!

Xavier and Jérôme come out to explore the surroundings in the darkness, losing their way amid the winding narrow streets, going in circles, the call of the muezzin echoing back to the white walls. Everywhere, they observe the bullet holes through the façades. Coming back to the villa, they see Dzana standing over at the balcony, smoking, smiling. Xavier smiles too. She feels alone, so hosting allows breaking the monotony of lonely hours. Xavier heads to the room and slumps onto his bed staring at the ceiling while Jérôme comes to chat with Dzana.

– Where is your friend?

– Crashing on the room. So, what do you do to take your mind off things? She scrutinizes him. A cloud of smoke gets out of her mouth. The atmosphere is singular, captivating.

– You know what? Life is unfair, really. I'm in good shape and look at me. I'm alone with my sick father. You stand by me, couchsurfers passing through stand by me. But most of the time I have nobody to talk with. Jérôme feels uncomfortable.

– I tease you. Keep your cool. You know, I'm the kind of person who loves opening my life. What I enjoy the most is to encounter foreigners because I'm running out of money to travel. I have to be down-to-earth. One day, I fall in love with a couchsurfer. He was from Italia. He stayed one week but he ended up postponing his departure. We spent one month together until we realized that it was impossible for him to set up here. This country, this situation jeopardized our chance, you know what I'm saying?

– What did you do?

– What I think first? If it is this kind of love my mom used to warm me about, I'm in real big trouble!

– Ahah!

– You got anything to say Man?

– Nothing!

The wrinkles make her even more attractive.

– I'm not intending to stay here. Next year I plan to travel, first in France. So I hope to see you two guys?

– Of course.

– By the way, did you enjoy the city?

– It was dark, a little bit empty.

– Be careful, the Western are considered as Walking Dollars. Don't talk too much, and obviously, talking about politics or religion stuffs is dangerous to be upfront.

- So that you often travel in exotic locals?

–I love it! Make it up make it up for me and change the story! And it takes my mind off the things that stress me out.

– Why not Croatia?

– Croatian people? I have no truck with that. This tea sucks in a big way!

– Which perfume do you like the most?

– What are you talking about?

– Your tea...

– That soothing, magical formula called papaya cream from Brazil.

– Well, dog my cats!

– Yeah... Besides, I'm particularly fond of Brazilian tea. I've been twice in this country, and I couchsurfed.

- Eat your heart out.

Dzana stares at him. She hangs back.

  –Cuddle up and be my little clinging vine, handsome boy. We're spiritually inclined.

  –Like we siamese twins connected by our brains.

Jérôme goes to her, she's letting him stroke her hair, he embraces, caresses,...

Jérôme and Xavier are seeing the sights, dawdling around. Meanwhile, Dzana is checking a website.

– Guys, when is your bus for Split tomorrow?

– At 11pm.

– Ok, I found out...so I can propose you to drop you off halfway between our two locations. That way we have time to visit some clean uncrowded beaches alongside the coast.

– Wow, you are so kind Dzana. Are you sure?

– No problem, you know I start working at 6pm. First I can bring you to a nice sidewalk café near the beach in which they serve incredible breakfasts, you'll see by yourselves.

Immediately afterwards we can go to a beach near the border of Croatia.

– I'm ok with that. However I want to invite you.

– Take it easy. I'm happy to invite you. You are my guests. Furthermore, you are my best guests.

– Wow, you'll make me blush! says Jérôme.

– Hosting cost you, right? asks Xavier.

– Yes, a lot. I should slow down. It's the reason why I think about taking a short break after you. Things are not so great, my contract's up at the end of the season.

Indeed, the beach with fine sand is empty. Dzana is scrambling over the rocks where the waves are surging over.

– Come on!

Jérôme and Xavier struggle against the wind and sit.

– It is wonderful. I use to come here before I work. It's so restful, I like it.

– You often come with couchsurfers?

– Of course! Except my brother who visits me sometimes, only couchsurfers come with me.

– Do you often feel alone?

– Yes and no. I have a big family, several cousins but they don't have spare time because most of them are shop keepers or retailers. So I strive to manage my time between my job, my friends and my father. And it's tricky.

Xavier wakes up and feels backache because of the burden trip he carried out the day before. He drags his feet scratching his head. He doesn't figure out that Jérôme is out when he hears his voice. He opens the door and sees his friend with Dzana laughing on the balcony.

– Hey guy, come on! You sleep too much!

– You didn't sleep?

– Not so much. We talk all night long. Jérôme told me about your girl who is in turmoil since you surf.

– Gossip...dramas of all kind, the highs, the lows, unconditional love...harsh reality.

– Liar! I know the story. But you have to understand her position. She doesn't know what happens during your trip maybe because she's not open-minded? But you have better to take a bold decision. You say to her: believe me or leave me!

This last sentence sets off laughers.

– Trust me. Otherwise, this situation will undermine your relation. She has to accept that you can manage between your love story and your travels. Are you eager to explore the world? Yes? Come with me. No? Let me go.

– She's wonderful, right? says Jérôme.

– Tell her about the heart-warming experiences you live. Perhaps you could change her mind. She will be more easy-going, believe me. Women are all the same. We need to be reassured.

– That's how I like to run things. I had tried to keep her from what she was about to see. Why should she believe me?

– As funny as it be by you, it not that complex. Otherwise if she packs a gun you'd better run fast.

A silence creeps along. Dzana breathes in deeply and hugs Jérôme, a tear rolling down the chick.

– I'm going to miss you all, that for sure.

6

Manhunt.

Hi Jérôme,
I hope everything is doing well.
I'm coming to Paris soon. I'm going forward to see you there!
Send my loves to Xavier,
Dzana.

   – Greaaaaat! Glad tidings, welcome!
Xavier has been listening to your reasoning; it makes no sense at all.
   – She keeps paging me... says Xavier.

Hello Jérôme,
My name is Noah. I am Colombian. I go to Paris and I stay 3 days. I need someone to help me.
I don't have any problem with the cats.
Cheers.

   – Copy-past. Where did he see a cat? Pfff. Moreover he didn't mention the keyword.
   – Which one? asks Xavier.
   – "Mortadelle". I added it at the end of my profile. Thus, I can select or dismiss those who didn't take the time to read my profile.
   – Great!
And Jérôme to send the request to the trash.

Hi,
Ukrainian boy looking for a couch for 2 nights. Easy-going and open-minded.
Best regards,
Vladimir.

– No interest. Totally impersonal.

And Jérôme to send it to the trash.

At this moment, a pop-up window appears on the screen. It's their coming Spanish wacky host Pedro who wishes to chat up.

– *Wazzzzup guys?*

– Shit...

Moment of hesitation...then Jérôme makes an effort.

– *Like clockwork...*

Second moment of hesitation. A minute goes by, Pedro keeps the conversation going.

– *What are you doing?*

– *Nothing interesting. I'm answering to a request from an Ukrainian girl.*

– *Will you accept her?*

– What a curious guy. He's itching?

– Write this: Mind your own business, says Xavier.

Third moment of hesitation...

– *Are you here?*

– *Yes. No. I won't. The message is impersonal...*

Fourth moment of hesitation...

– *Why?*

– *As I already said, the message is impersonal. She didn't even mention my name.*

– *You should integrate a code into your profile. You add it at the bottom of your page. Thus, you demand that it appears in the request.*

– *Yeah that's smart. So Pedro I have to go, I'm going to take a shower.*

– *Turn on the webcam...*

Last moment of hesitation...

– *I'm kidding!*

Your message wasn't sent. Your interlocutor logged out.

Xavier knocks the door. A swearword perfectly audible comes from inside. Benicio opens the door of the upscale villa of Grenade.

– Get out of here! He bellows to the dog.

Dressed in a warm bathrobe, hairstyle of an apostle, the lifeless orbits deepen, he smiles, offering an upper jaw full of rotting teeth. The eyebrows spread out like compound bows. The wrinkles in the forehead show up when he raises his eyebrows. Three young guys face him. A hell of a cast: a kind of runaway Afro girl with a capillary scaffold making moon eyes, surrounded by two sporty-looking boys. The finest, the very best, the French cream...

The afternoon starts with friendliness and good humor. Benicio is courteous, the flat is comfortable and the guests feel secure...until the dinner comes. Classified as "not enough easy-going", Xavier didn't find favour with Benicio who not even deign to speak to him. He starts conversation with Albertine who, in the opposite, seems to curry some favor with him.
– Where are you from, sweetheart?
  – This kind of misogynous patois blasts a hole into my ears, to be honest... hits back Albertine, with a glass of sangria.
  – Let's drink to it! She gets balls! Come on, talk to me, you little punk.
El Rais has an advice for her:
  – Sweetheart, inside my house, it's necessary to have my backing, right?
Ironical as it may sound, he is talking about this shack. Anyway, Albertine cools down insofar as the wine takes effect. She feels the need to drain a bottle so she goes to the kitchen where she finds Jérôme who already passed one over.
– I'm just really bloody scared of him.
– So I'll give you the bottle to cheer is up a bit.

It's a sun-filled morning. His Majesty the King of Cordoba is upset. His obligees are at the mercy of his mood swings if they don't succumb to whims. His disdain is growing when Albertine knocks the jug over getting the pancakes cooked by the King wet; a crime of lese-majesty. Because of her blunder, she's repudiated, felting the sting of Benicio. Even though she hastens to clean up the table, he writes her off. He looks daggers; any facial muscle move.
  – Soot all over the place, you clumsy fool!
At this time, King's subjects figure out that they transitioned out of a moderated submission state in a slavish state. Even the King's favorite

switched from glory to disgrace. Standing by and watching this humiliating scene, Xavier looks at him in tight-lipped disapproval.

– I don't know who you think you are? You have no power of ownership! We are not in the 19th century anymore! Perhaps, some guests swore allegiance but as far as I'm concerned, I plan to maintain my autonomy, says Jérôme.

– That takes the cake! It is my house so you had better to play by the rules! Clean up the table! rails Benicio against Jérôme.

– You... dictator, you disgust me!

– Carry out! And you have to know that your response must be much braver. You react like a girl!

– What's the problem with girls? asks Albertine.

The tyrannical king administers a royal spit in the air each time he opens the mouth. Albertine, mad with rage, doesn't cool off.

– Picture this: I will slap your face... I am going to spank you...

She stands up abruptly, aims a blow at him so strongly that he falls over. In his fall, the left hand of Albertine pulls out three strands of hair, then she brandishes her trophy straight after. A trophy that she will auction off in Liberia. She takes the cheese and puts it inside his mouth. El Rais nearly to suffocate. The fallen King straightens his back in time to receive a nuclear explosion in the crotch. Albertine takes her things followed by Jérôme and Xavier and shuts the door.

In the crowded lit pedestrian streets of Sevilla, many curious people came to admire Easter celebrations. It's hard to go ahead. Albertine is bullied by a father whom the disabled son has been hit by her backpack.

Above all, it's hard to go ahead because at every corner you find the same mountain of men dressed with white hoods and same tunics. At a street corner, they find the building which faces up a basket court. In the third floor, Xavier rings. A piercing cry from inside is heard. Pedro, 54, stocky man looking trendy, in Hawaiian shirt sleeves jumps into his arms. He is pretty short and ecstatic, speaking with a marked Chinese accent. A cigarette in his left hand, he invites his guests to join the living room. Jérôme catches some words. Around the table, four young guys are eating a pizza.

– These are my nephews! says Pedro laughing.

– Nice to meet you, says Albertine, setting off laughers.

– Of course not woodcock! They are couchsurfers!

And Pedro points the finger towards their backpacks in total shambles.

First, Pedro has ants in the pants. Then he stands still in place of the father of a family, arms outstretched on each side of the table. He admires his children that smug look on his face, giving Albertine the creeps. There is Mika, 22, from Peru, Gary, 26, from Hungary, Simon, 21 and Antony, 25, both from Canada. Jérôme notices quickly that Pedro starts getting these nervous tics, you know, funny little cough. Pedro flails all around the table, going wild out, ending up sitting down and breaking a chair leg. Damn...the fall is violent. The guys become alarmed.

– Oooh! Pedro, what the hell happened?! Tabarnak! Did you hurt your coccyx?

After diner, the intriguing fellow proposes to live it up without consulting the group.

– Everybody out!

Already this behavior results in two main groups: on one hand the young, on the other hand, the old with twisted mind. Actually, the young are exhausted and dream about sleeping in a twin-size bed. Unfortunately, Pedro doesn't think about it.

– The old calls the shots, right? Start of the nightmare, mokes Albertine. There's something leaking in his mind...

In the hummer, Antony the tall is sitting on the passenger side, eyes shut, battery dead. But the passion of his neighbor and the way he drives shakes him like a rag doll. A real combination of offences: disturbance at night, making a lane change without the indicator, speed limit exceeded, going through a red light, busted seat-belt... He couldn't care less about the aftermaths. Albertine smiles.

– I'll tell you, there is no adventure more harrowing than riding shotgun with Pedro.

– Yeah girl! I'm so excited!

It's up to him to decide when his offspring will go to bed. He parks outside the large building where a Flamenco party takes place. Inside, middle-aged men and women are partying their asses off. It's 3am. The guitarists play hard the strings. Pedro wants to wake up Jérôme, he grabs him by the neck and gives him a dribbling kiss on the cheek. Jérôme stands up and pushes Pedro back.

– Burk. Let me alone.

– It's only the beginning, says Antony ironically.

Xavier heads to the back of the room, joined by Albertine. Both are ever been so close in the agony.

– Did you notice how dreadful this guy is? If he tries to touch me…

– Don't worry Albertine, you are a girl…

The seven Dwarves gather in a bench, waiting for the shutting. Pedro keeps on spinning around.

– It's pathetic, look at him… points out Albertine aloud, knowing that the old will never approach her.

– With Adele, it's our first time birthday. I don't know what to buy.

– About your birthday? Don't give Adele nothing. Buy yourself something: jumper cable, leather shoes, a box of cigar… wrap it up, give it to her. She's gonna hate it and give it right back. That way, the day she dumps you, you won't be without nothing!

– Damn, you're so smart…

It's 5am. Everybody squeeze up in the hummer. The giant Canadian guy starts conversation with Pedro, getting on Albertine's nerves.

– Look, this guy is totally peace and love. Although he is dead tired, he talks with the old. Look at the way he sucked up. What do you expect? Sleeping in his bed? Keep crawling, let it be!

Albertine and Xavier can't stop giggling. Pedro speeds up, turning on the music at his top level, almost blowing up everyone's eardrum, except Mika who is sleeping in the rear. The bright moon soaks into the clouds, the werewolf looks in the rear-view mirror. His eyes are the eyes of Michael Jackson in *Thriller* video clip. He is the only one laughing. Albertine stares at him. This man seems to turn into a wolf when there is a moon. But now it's almost dawn, the birds sing, people go out. A moment of clarity wakes Jérôme up.

– Do you know where we gonna sleep? Did you see some mattress or bed?

In the apartment, Pedro throws three air mattresses on the floor. Albertine jumps in the sofa bed.
   – Simply pump your mattresses guys.
   – We need a pump Pedro.
   – I don't have it. Sorry. Try with your mouth.
   – Really? It's gonna be hours!
   – Do you have the choice Jérôme?
The guys waste the pumping because the device is out of service.
– My nerves are shot!
But after many unsuccessful attempts, Pedro brings a hairdryer.

Jérôme has trouble falling asleep. Albertine has trouble too. She would like to talk to him concerning Pedro, the way he got handsy with them all day long. She observes the stars throughout the bay window. She feels anxious at the idea of spending two more nights here. Pedro turned out to be much worse than expected.
She peeks over the sofa. She would like to stand up and get closer to Jérôme but the guys are all balled up on the ground, except Mika and Gary who were the first guests to arrive so they share the king size bed with Pedro. She ends up falling asleep.

Shortly after is when the chaos ensues. They wake up to a tremendous sound. Albertine is lying face downwards on the sofa, the head on the pillows, remaining unruffled. Much to their amazement, an amount of churros is spread out on the table and the Canadian guys are already tearing down the foods with their canines. All is eaten in a flash. Jérôme, who is in the background, finds this show sickening.
   – All I can focus on is their shit breath. I'd sooner starve to death than join them.
The invader approaches him and touches his hair. He picks the wrong card. Jérôme pushes him back while the scavengers are too occupied with the foods to see this preposterous scene. Albertine keeps an eye open. She rants at him.
   – Dirty old man...
Imperturbable, says Pedro loudly:

– Guys, listen. This morning, me, Mika and Gary are going to visit the Universal Exhibition downtown. Who wants to join us?

Once evening had fallen, the landowner says to his stewards who are laid down in the sofa, all obsessed by the basketball match:

– I suggest you to watch a DVD, ok? You are too quiet.

Then he slinks away. He comes back in his underwear, you think the worst. But no one takes a keen interest to his speech. Anyway, he turns on the TV, turning the volume up and slips away. A porn movie appears on the big screen. Firstly, nobody pays attention to it. But quickly Jérôme keeps his eyes up, screwed up about something strange, followed by Gary and Mika.

– Oooooh! What's the fuck!

– Tabernane Pedro! What the fuck it is? They yell in chorus.

They can not believe what they are looking at: hidden behind the glass wall, Pedro smiles and jumps, clapping his hands.

– Look at your faces guys, it's so funny!

– I think it's time to sleep... says Xavier.

– You're right, adds Antony .

Albertine stays on her sofa bed while the Canadian and French guys lay on the ground. Mika and Gary join the room where they have the honor sharing the bed with Pedro who already dreams. They stare at him with disgust. They lay down on both sides, staying still, staring at the ceiling, sleeping with one eye while Pedro sleeps like a log, until snoring make the situation unbearable. Gary stands up, followed by Mika. They both take their pillows and blankets, joining the living room, letting Pedro alone and shakes the wall.

Jérôme drags his friends out of bed.

– Hurry up, stop dawdling! We have to go... I hope we can slip away before he notices.

This morning it's the same old tune. Pedro is as excited as yesterday, touching the heads, the shoulders. However, everybody leaves except the French guys. Pedro gives a hug to Gary but his attempt with Mika fails.

– Good bye guys, I'm going to pick up someone.

– We must not let that opportunity slip away!

He mounts his scooter. Meanwhile, Jérôme takes the opportunity to rummage among the mess and ends up finding the laptop. He reminds the code pin and logs in. They agree on a path forward: leave the place. He sends a quick message to Iga, their next host in Lisboa. He begs her to accept them one day before.

Albertine stands in the balcony, soaks up the sun. She is nervous and edgy, still chain-smoking. Soon, however, Pedro is back from the station joined by a young American boy. Jérôme jumps and logs out.

– Pedro, we have to go now.

– Why?

– Our next host just sent a message. She changed her plan.

Jérôme strives to sugar the pill by offering a wide range of paintings of Paris.

   – Which one do you prefer?

Pedro stares at him, hesitates:

– So?

– I choose you, pushing the chest of Jérôme with his finger. What do you think about holidays we could spend together, you and Xavi? Why not on the beach?

Xavier offloads his obligations while Albertine's heart skips a beat.

– Not anytime soon...

Lisboa, Azuléjos, the displays of local earthenwares, colored façades, linen at the windows. From Bairro Alto to Marques de Pombal, the old ladies stand in the balconies. Rua Belem, Sagres is popping between two pasteis de nata. In the oven of the passenger compartment, Iga is driving, Behind the sunglasses, she looks like class, smart, self-reliant.

– What happened over there, in Sevilla? I myself am a very keen advocate for finally taking serious measures to combat the deviant behaviors.

– Do you really must know?

– In fact, it intrigues me. Let's go home and you tell your mommy.

They realize later on that the girl who bores right is the sister. She's doing her manicured nails and remains silent. Does she speak English? In Portugal, every young people speaks English fluently. She stamps her feet and hums the charts on the radio. Meanwhile, Iga looks at the rear view mirror and overtakes a driving-school car using strong language that the

French guys can't catch. The way she drives reflects her personality, right down, frankly. She puts the wheel hard down and brushes against an old man in the car park of the residence of Amadora. They all squeeze inside the lift, except Xavier and Esmeralda who go upstairs. Albertine extricates herself and joins the fly guy. Esmeralda makes an about-turn and gets into the lift.

In the stairwell, Albertine drags her feet.

– Who does she think she is?

– Stop blustering, there are ten floors left.

On the floor the door is half open, inside Jérôme and the family including the new Iga's boyfriend are laid down on the sofa watching the Voice while eating crisps. Albertine is on the background admiring the painting: four strangers who barely know each other and who are giggling in front of a stupid broadcast!

Some because they are fans, others because they don't catch any word. After that Iga shows us around.

They will sleep on mattresses. There is a notebook too on which they are encouraged to leave a short message concerning their journey in Lisboa.

– Yeah, I'm an ambassador for *Couchsurfing*. I've been vouched for more than twenty times.

– Say it again?

– 'Vouched for' means I got a label of quality as a host.

– Sure... so at worst you can report Pedro? asks Jérôme.

– Somehow, you are a kind of...ghostbuster? adds Albertine.

– Of course, to the administrator who will ban him. We have to crack down on him. Never pass up!

– Read this Jérôme, it's so funny, says Albertine.

Iga takes a look.

– Ok, what an incredible story; this guy was from India. He was supposed to arrive at noon. But actually he knocked the door in the middle of the night demanding a shower and a ready-made meal. I let him stay but at dawn he had to leave the house.

– Really?

– Last year I hosted a couple from Guatemala. They left all day long and came back at night with a garbage bag full of clothes, still pullin' ho's.

They piled everything and then off they went. Last month they requested me again, it was during the same period. They said ´we love your home, we want to stay one month with you!' I ended up figuring out their monkey business. It was all about wholesale trade and my flat turned into a warehouse! My answer was 'continue and I'll report back to the administrator who will ban you definitly, business men'.

Iga returns to the lounge. She sits out there in some armchairs and listens carefully the story, drinking herbal tea and giving herself a foot rub.

– Ok, a quick recap of our top stories, starts Jérôme. So weird. Our host was at once kind and a stickler, doing things to excess. I could say that especially during the evening it was tricky. My inmates and I couldn't know how to conduct themselves because he was our host. He dragged us out to a dancing all night long then we couldn't sleep.

– It is starting to sound like a stalker, she says.It has nothing to do with your journey-related behavior, nothing whatsoever. That means you don't have to accept what your host is and all that goes with it, to agree to do stuffs for him just because he thinks he wears the trousers and the young guys are little submitted boys. And all things considered, you should leave a negative reference. Should you?

– The problem is that if I leave a negative reference, he can dishonestly leave a negative one too. Most of people strive to avoid conflict.

– I know that the system has to be enhanced but things have changed Jérôme. Keep up with what's going on! Now, your host will see what you left only when he leaves a reference himself. In other words, he can't be dishonest with you insofar as he can't anticipate your feelings. Simply put, be free, don't feel embarrassed.

– We learnt from it. To say the truth, we just checked how many positive references he got on his profile.

– How many?

– 72 positive, 0 neutral, 0 negative.

– Guilty is still at large, running away! adds Albertine.

– Well, he's bipolar, clinically depressed and a mendacious dirt bag, cuts off Albertine.

– I think you're being a little overdramatic, tempers Jérôme. He behaved properly until this moment.

– Which moment? asks Iga.

– When he broadcasted a porn movie!

– Ai que horror! To okropne as we say in Poland. I compel you to testify! This guy kind of drifted into a werewolf as you said. You must read between the lines. Sometimes, people leave a positive note, but what they write inside the message is not glorious. So first, be careful, be serious. Second, fulfils your duty by leaving a negative reference which warm others surfers. And step by step, these guys are erased from the website. And after what could happen if nothing is done? Some guys could pounce around butt neaked!I'm an ambassador of Couchsurfing. Give me his profil, I can provide feedback to the administrator.

– You could?

– Of course! His profil will be deleted within 48 hours and he is going to lose all his benefits!

That very evening, everybody go to bed quickly; the husband because he's dead tired, Iga because she's up early, Esmeralda because she's too shy to stay alone with strangers. But she doesn't bow out as far as she sleeps on the sofa.

In the middle of the night, Xavier, who stayed awake, hears a noise coming from the saloon. So he opens the door a crack, catches a shadow flashing by but when he scans the dark saloon, it's empty. He turns back and faces Esmeralda.

– You don't sleep?

– What do you care? No peeking!

– Oh, sorry Madame... How is your life?

She whispers.

– Listen, I have something for you. I don't want your number, I don't want to give you mine and I don't want to meet you nowhere. To summarize, I don't want none of your time. You're a guy that can't get no love from me.

– No woman, no cry, right?

– Exactly...

She slips away with a slight sneer. Xavier jams the main door with a socket and climbs out onto the roof. He bends over. The entire district is sleeping. He goes down the twelve floors of stairs and goes for a ride, blowing oranges off the trees, loitering in the boulevard, rehashing the last argument he had with Adele, dwelling on the past. That's good timing, a grocer's shop is open. He sticks his hand in his pockets and finds enough coins to take his mind off his troubles. Bad patch...

What's the time? It's entirely dark in there. Jérôme and Albertine are no longer here, so Xavier realizes that they are all together in the saloon. Shit...obliging, he doesn't think anymore, what happened this night is meaningless.

In the saloon, it is exactly what Xavier foresaw; the sisters are together on one side, facing Albertine and Jérôme.

- Hey Xavier, we're waiting for you! Before breakfast it's morning prayer, says Iga with a huge smile.

However, Esmeralda is already stuffing herself with franceshina.

– Stop making a pig sister...we have guests.

Esmeralda stares at Jérôme with a fair and square smile and whispers a word in Iga's ear who immediately sets off a tense laughter. Xavier bubbles up.

– You got agita bro? says Esmeralda.

– No, look at him, he's kinda cool. Anyway... Ugh, may we join hands for grace? Bow down please. Oh God, it's your child. Thank you so much, we are all alive this morning, we're healthy, fortunately, thanks to you and your greatness. Oh God, we're mourning those who died during the night, those who are suffering today and those who are starving. You bless us with this breakfast on our table and we all want to thank you for. Please, make the trip of my friends safe. Amen. Enjoy your breakfast my dear friends and after we're going forward to visit the surroundings.

The lagoon and the salt pans surround the city where the main canal overlooks. On the sea front, myriads of multicolored houses spread out. Three old people on deckchairs are resting, appreciating the emptiness of the spot.

– You made me cry with laughters. You are so different each other but nevertheless you travel together. It's crazy but in the same time so beautiful.

– She follows us actually, answers Xavier. She has no professional liability.

– And you have no conjugal liability, replies Albertine.

– Albertine rubs off on us, says Jérôme.

– Oh don't have an argument because of me guys! It was a joke. So, time goes by so fast. These two days went by in a flash. I'm going to miss you, really. You should come back next year and we could practice windsurf during an entire week, my cousin is the club owner!

– I'm counting on it, says Jérôme.

– We are likely to do so.

Iga drops them off at the artisanal fishing port which leads to the station. Iga parks alongside the boats colored from stem to stern. She warmly kisses her friends and stares at them going away. She gets on the car. Engine starts. Albertine sees her in the mirror, mourning, tears rolling down her chicks. Never look back, she turns the wheel.

7

Upright men.

Jérôme is sitting at his desk while Dany is lying on his table. Diego is standing on the bottom. He is busy slamming the closet, until broken.

– Not to say he's good at it, but it keeps him busy.

Jérôme observes the scene, astonished.

– They call it the court of miracles...

He looks through the drawer and finds a book inside.

– So, guys, if you are interesting in resolving equations today, tell me.

– We've just been through three hours of music. Now, I just want to buy my scooter, says Dany.

– Ok, but you need money. And to get it you have to...

– Work? I know this song.

– What are you waiting for?

– Because I was told that I'd get my college certificate this year, which I didn't. Look I'm way past caring.

– What happened?

– Ask the Principal. That bastard, he wouldn't even leave me that.

– Cool...

– We also know that the closet is bursting with primary school books.

– That's why you lock the door! yells Diego.

Dany turns out to the other table and raises it above his head, flipping the table upwards, many times, under the gaze of his teacher.

– He's so ugly, I can't stand it. Shoot! They're savages who only act by instinct... It is imperative that I get rid of this situation as soon as possible.

Dany laughs. He is temporarily insane. Then suddenly, somebody knocks on the door. It's the director. He looks frail, innocent, rather puny.

– The inspector wants to see you. The rumor I heard was, you were thinking of leaving us, applying for another position.

– Yep... euh no. Do I have to answer right away? Eh, why are you staring at me like that? No, it's brilliant down here, I'm loving it.

– That feels good to me. But what on earth are they doing?

– They do not want to work.

A pencil case flies past his face at about 50 centimetres.

– Well, I'll just let you get to work. Good luck.

The director runs away. Jérôme checks the time.

– We have thirty minutes remaining. I have an idea. Let's go to the computer center. I'm also going down there to send a request.

The bandits rush out and shoot the door. Jérôme follows behind. He connects to Couchsurfing and looks for a Canadian host. He filters the last connected profiles and stumbles across a couple from Saguenay-Lac-Saint-Jean area. The girl in the picture wears big glasses.

– Is that not the Canada at his best?

It's just a few days ahead of Spanish trip. This Friday afternoon, the entire classroom of the Building and Public Works Institute is full of CEO. Eight out of ten are sleeping arms crossed, one is drawing Xavier on his slate, and one lady crumples the lecture note up and throws it on Xavier's buttocks while he is writing on the board, triggering burst of laughers. Going through an intense week of training has been so exhausting, climbing some scaffolding and painting the walls...Xavier who is in a rotten mood is astonished. It's scarcely believable. Xavier, ex naughty boy, getting knocked about a bit by CEO who misbehave. At first beside himself, he regains self-control and checks the corridor letting his boss through. He closes the door slowly and confesses:

   – I don't subscribe to this project. You're here to have fun, you don't
   need to solve problems that you can delegate to executives in reality. To
   be honest, we don't get along with the boss, he's selfish and doesn't care
   about training staff. The only reason I'm here is to have a steak in my
   plate.

The phone vibrates in his pocket. It's a message from Adele.

The secretary stands up and puts her hand in Jérôme's forearm. He's deep in thought. She shakes him. He reacts. The inspector is waiting for him on his office. In the lift, Jérôme looks at himself in the mirror. What's wrong?

Why is he looking for being confident? At the floor, the light from the office makes him nervous.

Inside, he is petrified by the stately behavior of the inspector.

– Sit down.

The inspector rummages in a stack of files.

– So, you ask for a transfer; you are interested in leaving the Department of Education? You see, there is a lot of kinda people. You know what kinda is? You kinda want a career change, you kinda want to get in shape, you kinda want to get a straight-A...

– Yeah, I run out of room to grow and I've developed a passion for travel. I like to understand how a country works. I would like to take part in the links between France and his partners.

– This is commendable.

The inspector takes a break, touching his felt hat.

I have something for you concerning the Foreign Affairs Department, more specifically theEuropean Affairs.

– Perfect. It's my speciality.

– Be modest. There is a huge gap between visiting a country and understand how it works... Good luck.

It's 2am. Jérôme is awakened by a latch sound coming from the saloon. A baseball bat on his back, he goes ahead. What he sees doesn't make him feel better. So he seizes a brush and pushes the window. Xavier is outside with poor suspension. He surely went out the neighbor's window. With trembling hands he tries to push the window with his left foot, in vain...

   – Don't look down, it's a long, long way to fall.

Jérôme seizes his arm and pulls him from the fall.

– Nobody died, fortunately!

– You get into bad ways buddy. What are you doing outside?

– Better batten down the hatches. Not a single word to Adele.

– I'm your buster Xavier. Trust me.

– It's your sister.

At exactly the wrong time, Xavier is apprehended by Adele who emerges from the room, bumping into the sofa where Mika sleeps.

   – Who is this guy?

– It is Mika, we have met him on a trip to Spain before where we were both guests at a house.

– Anyway...Where did you hang out again? I fed up with your soft shots. You keep on acting like a fool!

– Leave me alone, my head is spinning...

– Please, the only thing I want from you is to be up front about your travels. And I will never back down on the issue.

– I am deeply sorry that you seem confused. You may think I'm a player but you're completely lost. You're brother is the best witness, right?

– Are you kidding me? Do I look foolish? My brother, you should use him as a pattern! Your silly game I won't allow!

Jérôme smiles.

– You want to know my opinion? At this time, I see no happiness in your own life, so you act out all your jealousy. Who are you to say that I'm living wrong, always telling me what to do!

Xavier shoves her and she loses her balance. He slams the door while Adele handles with breath-holding spell. Jérôme hugs her.

– Maybe he feels better abroad, and coming back here makes him feel sad. You can't help it.

– Life with him is like a coin; you never know if you are on reverse side and everything's fine or if you are on front side right in your face!

She stands up and rushes towards the bathroom. She leans on the sink and she looks deeply into a face which is fallen from grace. Her eyes red from the sadness make her even less desirable.

On this gloomy morning, Jérôme logs in.

– Xavier, come on. Mika and Gary left a positive reference to Pedro! It reminds me the lyrics of Ana about Jin-Sang story. These guys will keep on doing shady stuffs as long as people leave positive references.

– Most of surfers don't take the time to read those who put boots on the ground, hastening to send a copy/paste. Who's to blame?

– They have their share of responsibility.

Wailing and cry of rage from Jérôme's room stop the conversation. The door is half open. Kneel down, a Japanese girl is sniveling in front of her laptop.

– She's skyping with her boy. Yesterday, she did the same, staying locked
up. Hysterical...
The girl keeps still a moment, then she turns the head, stares at them
coldly and finally turns away. She restarts hollering at the laptop. The
neighbor starts yelling: "Say to your Chinese to shut it up!"

8

Getting around.

– What! yells Jérôme.

– Why do you need to bellow like that? says Xavier.

– It's Fukima. She left me a neutral reference!

– Did she explain the reason?

– She complains of our lack of availability! She adds that she had to visit Paris by herself.

– We are not a travel agency! I can't believe it, punished for being righteous!

In his mailbox, a message from Walter appears.

Hi Jérôme,
I will be glad to host you in Florida. I just want to question you about a detail; what happened with your last surfer? Why did he leave a neutral reference?
Thanks in advance.
– Walter.

-If you can't read, ask your daughter.
Message deleted.

– No, I would never say that...

In this afternoon, the main place where is located the City Hall of Trois-Rivières is crowded. Children are playing with the fountain, a flock of retired are going Riverdance. Jérôme and his mates are on a bench reading the plan. They must go outside the city and cross the bridge which leads to the North District.
Streets stretch over kilometers. They walk the avenue till their legs fall like stone. Weakened by the jet lag, Adele stops.
   – Hang on!
   – Hurry up, stop dawdling!

A young guy snacking on blueberries and walking like jumping jack is on the way. Jérôme stops him.

– Hey, we are lost. We're looking for a bridge.

The strange thing stares at him with big eyes which cover the half of the face.

– Eh! You are French? He asks with a very strong accent. I like you. I lived in Paris for two years and I've been blackmailed and beaten up in the subway.

– Thank you, you're about the only person who doesn't get a tattoo! notices Jérôme.

The guy laughs.

– Jeez! D'you see that! Here it's a lifestyle. Anyway, d'you know, I got some French blood. Your king Louis XIV sent my forefather 'sieur Boucher into Quebec in order to kick Indian's ass. It's effin' funny that I see them on the streets! D'you know, your king had the same accent that we have now, until we cut their head.

The French observe a one-minute silence after that. They let the guy speaks, he' s so funny. Only his mouth is on movement, not only to speak but also to swallow the blueberries.

– Effin' hell, Montrealers call us lumberjacks from the woods. They believe that we cut down the trees all day long and they don't catch our fuckin' accent.

The guy scrutinizes them, swallowing more and more blueberries.

– You're in short pants. Be careful, the mosquitoes want to suck the French blood out of you here. Slip pants on.

– Got it, thanks.

– D'you have a tank?

– No, as you can see, we rented those bikes .

– Okay, walk straight the lights, turn on the left and cross Fusey street, pass through Saint-Christophe Island. That's it. Bye!

– Thanks!

– You're welcome.

On the road, the French notice that the stop signs are written in French language, that KFC fast-foods are called PFK for Poulet-Frites du Kentucky. There is no indication that we are in North America except the perpendicularity of the streets. Canada is using locally sourced materials such as canvas, fur and wood for its home. Every squirrel in the parks bury their nuts and alert their buddies. Sitting on the luggage carrier, snuggled up to Xavier, Adele smiles when she sees Albertine arms up, pedaling at full speed. The width of that lane combined with a very limited amount of traffic going up and down bring a wind of freedom.

Ahead, the boastful Albertine is always very close to falling on either side. Adele is hugging Xavier as hard as she could. Her right cheek is sticking on his shoulder. She stares at the maple trees. And she barely lets herself breathe because she never wants that moment to end.

The little house on the corner is the destination. A husky with eyes different colors almost yanks the leash out of the stoop. Jean-Benoit holds the dog. An octopus has taken up residence on his head. He makes customized snowmobile. He is dressed like he is on Pimp my ride and stinks like an air freshener.

– Wheeeeeretooooo! I didn't see you coming, I was fixing a bike in my shed! It's a... It's a big fuzzy dog that you just want to pet.

– Hey! yells Adele.

– I sell this one 6600 bucks!

– Is it expensive? asks Jérôme.

– No, no, no. Anyway, it's a business. On some occasions I go camping during four weeks in the blueberry fields to pick berries as a way to keep a roof over their heads.

– Wheeeeeretooooo! yells Ann-Josie too. How is life? You okay now?

Jean-Benoit is 6 feet tall. Ann-Josie is only 5 feet tall and with those big glasses, it's hard to see her sweet face, with intelligent eyes.

– Come inside, says Ann-Josie. Make yourself at home.

In the living room, a bunch of guys has already taken their seats on the sofa full of dog hair. Ann-Josie introduces them.

– Hey guys, there are couchsurfers from France!

All around, there are reptile houses. Inside, snakes of all size flicker their tongue. Albertine's eyeball open wide. Jean-Benoit gives out *Bud light time* drinks to anyone who loves that.

– No thank you, says Adele.

– Your throat is dry! It reminds me a guy who worked with me at the factory and whom I squabbled with! One day he approached me. He didn't rinse his effin' mouth out since the day before. So the dryness attacked the bowels. At this moment, you grip there, and you position yourself with feet so you can use your dorsal muscles to hold your breath, tabarnane!

Everybody laughs. Ann-Josie intervenes.

– Quit swearing! Goddamn, goddamn... he always like to mingle.

– D'you see that! Mingle! Lol!

– Move on! Idiot!

– Wait, wait, I have to finish cooking the *boeuf bourguignon* and fried potatoes. Let's settle down!

Ann-Josie is wondering at something.

– Table's set, food's served, jesus!

– Hell no, you can relax, breathe! answers Jean-Benoit.

– We live like goddamn kings! Is it Versailles or what?

– Let's take a pic, hun!

– So, what's the occasion? asks Jérôme.

– In honor of your National day!

– I was not aware!

– What about you?

– We are teacher.

– Okay, big nerd, eh?

– We're on transit.

So there is Simon from Guadeloupe, Marianne his new blond, Maryline his ex whom the beauty went to crap. Sitting right in front of Jérôme, squeezing him. Maryline has only one goal: to get it. Jérôme strives to avoid eye-contact. Fortunately, Jean-Benoit makes the show.

– D'you know, we are a theatre company. In a short while, we'll perform Beauty and the Beast.

– Does everyone need an audition to get with you?

– Yes. Recently, three girls came.

Ann-Josie cuts him off.

– Hun, you gotta give context, put some meat around the bone!

– Stay outta my story, jeez! I'm a big boy, okay?

– Okay, but you forgot to say that you were at the microbar totally done.

– Yikes, mind your own! So three girls came. A tall, skinny, beautiful blonde. Another dressed up like a dog's breakfast. The last one, she's one...pretty gal. But goddamn, she sang out of tune! Whatcha' doing? I chocked on my own vomit, or somebody else's after I gulped down 40 Jack ounces!

Everybody laugh out loud except Ann-Josie who would prefer to hide under the table whereas Jean-Benoit is replaying the scene, making his flatwares fall.

– You pig! What's that you sayin'? People will gossip on their return to France. I know the drill. Anyway, my chum uses to crawl over there. We can go, it could have been the last act.

– Let's go! says Albertine getting excited.

Ann-Josie stares at Albertine.

  – Another shot?

  – Last one…

  – Cheers…

  – And you Jérôme?

  – No thanks.

  – We're celebrating! Damn straight. No holding back tonight! Be my effin' guest.

Simon stares at Jean-Benoit.

  – D'you mind, it reeks of smoke in here. The odor…smells stale. By the way, Jean-Benoit is quite a number. You never get bored with him. Not a dull moment.

Jérôme cuts off.

  – Can we ask you something Ann-Josie?

  – What?

  – I don't know…

  – Come on, you tease! You sneaky little tease!

  – It's dumb, forget it.

  – No, no, no!

  – Can we stay two more days?

  – Yes! But I didn't ask you Adele if you host people sometimes?

  – I created a profile. It was automatically on "can accept people". After 48 hours, I received 35 messages in my box. All from India and some of them were declaring their love for me.

  – Crazy whatchamacallit story, eh! Got yourself all dolled up on the picture?

Everybody laugh except the French who don't catch any word.

– Show your picture, asks Ann-Josie.

– You cute. Let do it!

– Thank you but I'm an old lady now...

– Noway, it's a pile of shit, says Marylin.

– Pile of shit, yourself! laughs Ann-Josie.

– That make sense, women are in minority in India! adds Jean-Benoit.

– You don't knowjack shit, it's not a reason! yells Marylin.

Ann-Josie cuts off Maryline.

– Me too. One day I posted a rather cute picture of me. Guess what? A guy told me that he was planning to cover the world just for me!

– I heard a story but I don't know if it's true... a guy who was looking his guests through an eye-hole between his room and the bathroom, comments Jean-Benoit.

– Out you go, boy! Tabarnane!

– It's sucks!

– I can't believe it!

– You naive Ann-Josie! says Marylin. Strange people are everywhere; on the street, theater, at work... they are maybe one over thousands but take time to read a profile!

A noise of a plastic bag disturbs sleep. Albertine doesn't dare to open the eyes, scared of losing sleep definitely. However, she feels something living alongside her body. A thing crawling. She can feel her deep breathe. This noise lasts some minutes. The thing stretches, sheds his skin, and disappears. She can hear a creacking that prevents her from sleeping. It comes from the next room where her friend Xavier made it up with his girl. She gets some peace of mind and after a while, she goes to sleep.

– Shall we sit outside? suggests Ann-Josie. It was a blast yesterday!

– So cool!

Spontaneously, a group of girls just sit down on the low wall beside the table, intrigued to see Quebeckers joined by French people.

– How did you meet each other? asks an overweight girl.

– Via *Couchsurfing*, answers the frail Ann-Josie. Come on in, get yourself a chair.

– It won't take long. Uh, how do you say?

– *Couchsurfing*. It's a social network. People host people...

– What's the point?

– Thus far you discover their lifestyle, it's fun, eh.

– Fine! I'll enroll in, that way I could host French people like you, I'm open and I got a couch! What's the deal?

– Okay, you register on the website, fill out your profile and add a picture.

– Could I ever! X'cuse...

Just in mid-sentence, the girl leaves and already gets a phone number of a chum on the table behind.

Ann-Josie and her best friend Sophie look at each other and laugh, on her ass.

– I'm open and I got a couch. She's very freethinking and forward, isn't she? Albertine repeats.

– Y'know, it doesn't mean that she spreads her legs to the highest bidder, a skank or stuff...in France you act like this but the rest of us it's not our type.

– Play it up, play it up... Gérard, we get tired of waiting! Sophie yells. By the way, what's your job in France?

– I'm teacher, says Jérôme.

– Eh! That's fun! I was interning at the primary school but I gave up quickly. Y'know, teaching wasn't my thing, but this lady was an artist with a chalk, she knew how to fascinate children.

The waiter shows up and holla at them. Ann-Josie stands up and gives him a peck.

– A wheat beer for me! starts Sophie.

– Two! adds Ann-Josie.

– Four! orders Xavier for Adele.

– Five! says Jérôme.

– Gin... follows Albertine.

– Okay. So fifteen piarces please!

– You French people it's okay? asks Ann-Josie.

  – By the way, your plan for tomorrow? adds Sophie.

Jérôme gives the thumbs up.

– We go to the eastern side to see the whales.

– Hitchhiking? Good luck! Hitchhikers aren't picked up. In Europe it works but in America it's not the lifestyle. Maybe if you are two girls or a chum with his blond. But in your case it won't do it!

– You will getting the run around! I let you use my chariot but come back at 4pm 'cause I have a class.

– You call it a car? Please, it's a lemon! laughs Sophie.

After consideration, Ann-Josie restarts:

– Now that I think about it... Jean-Benoit has to go to work tomorrow, the upshot is that with Sophie we thought you guys might like swimming in the lake if it is not pouring. Pack your swimsuit. Tomorrow it's swimming pool! I'll put the icebox!

The vulgar girl rounds up.

– U-turn, the bunch of floozies is back...

– Tongues will wag... whispers Sophie.

– Hey! Where d'you go?

– I saw a blast over there, so cute... anyway, I missed your sentence.

– Eh! I was telling that *Couchsurfing* is a lifestyle. You open your house, you trust people, you learn from others, and when people are fun, wow! The girl stares at Albertine.

– Oh, straight gin is so vulgar, my dear... oh, boy, are my pups growling.

– You are vulgar, look at yourself! yells Albertine.

– But it ain't vulgar, it's just...it's just the way I feel. Okay, okay...*Couchsurfing*...well... And if the boy is cheesy?

– Find an excuse! Shorten your trip.

– If he's a jerk double-crossing?

– It's like painting a goddamn bull's-eye on your ass! Say you're all in, and that your chum he's fuckin' done.

– I full agree with you! Okay...it was cool to talk to you, but I have to go. Bye!

– Wait, wait! Don't use it for that. It's not the point. You'll be sad, to be outspoken.

– Skeptics will be proven wrong...she says, chewing.

She goes manhunting. Ann-Josie speers at her.

– Shut up, dimwit. Get the shit out of it! You idiot! Goddamn that pissed me off!

– You kidding, right? asks Sophie.

– Well I never! She's missing the point. It is exactly this kind of pitoune who spoils the concept.

The jukebox plays loud the steel guitars of the country sisters. Adele grabs Xavier's arms and starts dancing the triple step. Jérôme and Albertine join, standing in second line. The lindy hop breaks out; Rock step, triple step, rock step, triple step...

The bus heading towards the airport is overcrowded. However, nobody drags a suitcase. Surprising...The countryside spreads out and the city disappears. Becoming aware of his mistake, Xavier rushes toward the driver who explains that he took the wrong way. Xavier and Adele disembark in the midst. The circumstances make clear the need to reestablish the situation. Not to mention that Adele is getting very irritable. Tinged with sadness, she incriminates Xavier:

– I'll miss my plane! Maybe it's fate? Maybe I shouldn't take it?

– Don't say that. They are waiting for you in Paris. Let's go! Your job is more important.

In a bad mood, she insists on questioning:

– How long do you stay in Florida? What do you plan to do?

– We expect to go home in one week.

– You'll get a lot of fun, for sure... with or without me it is the same for you.

– Let it down...

– You get on my nerves Xavier! It took me four years to know you, but now Albertine doesn't need to have me on. And Jérôme tells me fibs!

– You're freaking out a little bit!

Adele emphasizes.

– My brother takes sides with you, as usual!

– Keep your voice down!

– In this godforsaken place? Are you joking?

The coach pass us during the fight. Adele stands in the middle of the road. When she notices a white Porsche, she waves once. The car breaks. A young guy rolls down the window, blowing cigarette smoke straight into Adele's face.

– Please, I have to go to the airport. Could you take me there?

She realizes the guy is hefty and lets her admire his sweaty naked chest, and the dudes at the back are wearing the same outfit. It doesn't matter.

– What are you doing Adele? asks Xavier.

She doesn't pay attention.

– Help me, please. I'm desperatly late for the plane!

The guy turns to his dudes and smiles at them.

– Well, you have nothing to worry about. Hop in! But I only got one place, sorry...

Adele looks at Xavier.

– I'm sorry.

She steps inside. The *Porsche screeches* out of the driveway.

– You don't even know them... whispers Xavier.

The airport stretches out to infinity. How many counters? How many officers does she meet? Departing, outbound, inbound, everything's confusing.

– I'm stressed out and pissed off and I'm getting very mad!

– Sorry, Madame?

– I'm registered on the next flight.

– Ok, let me see... sorry, Check-in are closed concerning outbound flights.

– I have been running for one hour, please make an exception.

The officer stares at her.

– I just inform you about the Check-In Deadline : This is the time limit beyond which you can no longer check in for. Sorry but my advice for her is to buy another ticket.

– Are you kidding me? Just because I took the wrong way?

– Everything in this life is about details. Don't forget it.

– What are you jabbing about now?

Adele is mourning.

– I could never afford it! I'm going to be wildly out of control!

With grim determination, the officer stands firm.

– Madame, pay it or leave it. The line is growing. So, cash or charge?
Adele is stunned. What's the option? Get a job as a cleaning lady? In a fit
of rage, she kicks the terminal which bangs into the officer's face. People
on the line behind make such a hullabaloo about the aggression.
   – Call the supervisor!
The supervisor, a little woman, 50, goes and speaks to Adele:
   – This little slip of a woman has to make her mark in this harsh and
   violent man's world, right? Exceptionally, we accept you to embark in
   the next flight.
The officer behind the desk stands up and gets closer. She faces Adele.
They have roughly the same size.
   – Kidding aside, take notice that we've gotten rid of people for much
   less. Why am I denying myself the pleasure of smashing your head?

A light bump over the Montreal-Fort Lauderdale flight, the stewardess
makes an announcement quite casually.
In the airport, the queue stretches over 200m, each one waiting for
getting his picture taken.
Jérôme bumps into the stewardess, a beautiful Métis, leaning on a
counter, getting absorbed in her smartphone, taking the time to wink at
him.
Xavier copes with fulfilling the form. He reads aloud:
   Question 1: Are you conspiring to carry out a terrorist attack
   against the USA? No.
   Question 2: Are you planning to abduct a child in the US ground?
   No.
   Question 3: Did you take part to Nazi regime? I was not born...check
   my date of birth.
Jérôme, absorbed in his phone, cuts him off:
– Listen. I'm on a profile:

   *Read it carefully and entirely before request. I like the physical
   contact. I do like to take my guest in my arms. So nothing personal,
   it's my way of doing things.*

– Noway. Search someone else.

Going through the customs, the officer pries the form out of his hands.

– Address?

– Wait...

Xavier takes his phone and searches the address of the host.

– Jefferson Avenue.

– There is no hotel over there. Where do you couch?

– At a friend's house. We kept in touch online. He host us for free.

– And what does he get out of it?

– Absolutely nothing. It is called *Couchsurfing*. We meet new people who share their life, show us around and spend their time with us.

The officer stands up and talks to his colleagues, roaring:

Listen guys, they are going to couch at stranger's house, people found on a website!

The entire counter die laughing.

– Yeah, you don't know it... whispers Jérôme, striving to make them see sense.

The boats are docked at Marina alongside the shady walk where Palm trees are lined up in rows. On the edge of Marina is built the city of Fort Lauderdale; five days hard riding on horseback from Detroit. Right by the sea living districts with a lot of shops and bars spreads out. The city sprawls out from its seaside to Miami, which has an enormous surface area that extends upward into space. At the end of the boardwalk there is the Yatch of Walter easily identified by its specific shape, with an Irish flag flying high in the warm air. As a garden? A tremendous golf course that sounds like the same seen on MTV and right in the middle had been built a big artificial lake in which live various species. Facing that scenery, that tramp calling 911 on a ATM machine; damn crazy... Inside the boat, air-conditioning was installed. Walter is a wily old veteran with white on his head, having a string of couchsurfers flags from all around the world; more than 120 different flags. He is retired and spends his time traveling across the Atlantic. As a convinced patriot, he is arguing about a topical issue with two friends from the old guard.

Walter breaks off the conversation when he sees his new friends.

– Come on guys. Sit down. These are my friends, Arnold and Gerald.

One of them is like a freeze-dried prune, probably because of the sun.

– We still bicker about firearms.

– It's human being that triggers and kills people, not firearms, cuts off Walter. It's as if I blame forks for spreading overweight to the people. We are not going to ban forks to face with obesity!

– What's your opinion guys?

– Yet, it's people that pull the triggers, dares Albertine.

– Alright, it's not worth fighting, says Walter. We are always squabbling me and my homies.

– Walter claims that he stirs up more people in our association.

– Not stir up Gerald, recruit. You're losing head bro...

– What are you talking about? asks Albertine.

– We can assert at 90% that we are gay, so we have created an association for gay community in order to fight prejudice, the prune confesses.

– At your age, you don't know? That makes me wonder, dares Xavier.

– To say the truth, we belong to a club and we organize a party every Sunday.

This revelation is the opportunity to show his jaw with receding gums. A real baby face each time he opens the mouse.

– Here, we are deeply rooted in the gay district, definitely. We can go to a party this night, proposes Walter licking a shard of glass.

– Seriously?

– Yeah... don't be overcome, Walter answers, sticking out his tongue a bit between the teeth.

– Walter introduced us to the *Couchsurfing*. How long do you stay in Florida?

– Five days, answers Xavier snappish.

– Oh, where do you plan to stay the other nights?

– We didn't plan yet...

The old man turns towards Walter.

– They stay two nights at home?

– Yes. After I down the eastern seaboard.

– So you can stay in my spacious flat.

– Or at mine? trying to get ahead the prune.

– We'll think about it…

Flip-flop, Walter hastily changes the subject.

   – Guys, that's it. This mind-fuck is over.

In the velvet divans, an uptown-out of touch girl with dark pigtails is phoning. She wares a two-piece suit. She doesn't even pay attention to the strangers. She stands up, crosses Xavier, leaves the superstructure bridge and goes to the stern. She breathes in the sea air with her gaze fixes on the foam.

   – Tasneem, come say hello to my friends.

Her lips give a hint of an enigmatic smile. Her beauty is unmatched. She's mild-mannered. Such a great catch…

   – Hi, she simply says, keeping on phoning.

Walter goes on taking the grand tour. He shows them a 13m2 cabin wherein Albertine could sleep. Then he shows the cabin for guys. At last, he points out the jacuzzi shining in the sun.

– Don't you feel like takin' a dip Jérôme?

– It's yours guys!

He barely had time to talk that they dive headfirst. He is standing there with his arms folded. After a while he's up to the top and he locks himself away in his office. For a bit there, it looked like the architect built perfectly this room to enjoy the spectacular view on the jacuzzi. Hanged with the phone, Walter watches the fun begin. More than anything, he enjoys dominating. First, to that height he dominates the young, vertically speaking. Second, he dominates the needy because of his material wealth that he provides with.

That eye contact that lasts a bit too long, Jérôme intercepts it.

– I feel like we're getting weird look.

– Don't worry. There is the girl, don't forget.

Jérôme gets out of the pool and heads for the cabin.

On the boat, everybody sleeps. Xavier takes a look outside. He creeps across the superstructure until he joins the saloon where he beholds a subdued lighting. Tasneem is chilling out, reading something. She's got an

amazing tan. Xavier is eager to discover her. Not to mention this second
girl with plain face. Who cares!
He goes up to them and looks at Tasneem.

  – Any chance I might squeeze in here?
She stares at him and says half-heartedly.

– No problem. I was about to end.

– You live with your father?

– I know, I'm the daughter of a old man who brags about his money but
I'm lucky. I love living here. You see...not knowing where you're gonna be
one day to the next.

– Routine kills us...

The light close to her face unveils freckles hidden by the dark skin. Ah,
black hairs, wavy but not curly, right features, good teeth, labia minora.
Her cheeks have sharp contour and the hip size is perfect to roll some
dice on it. Her large mint green eyes could make all the men scream, even
her father. Yeah, that's the least you can say; her beauty is equal to
Dzana's and the game is gettin' deeper. On the other hand, the sister
Meryl is a bad copy of Scarlett Johansson; fatty girl, rasping voice, oval
face, plumper lips, crazy-fingernails, heavy make-up, ample bosom, vulgar
way to chew, ogling at him. Suddenly, someone from the background
approaches. It's Jérôme.

– Can I sit?

– Where? asks Xavier.

– Of course, answers Tasneem.

– What are you reading?
Xavier cuts him off.

– You're interested in literature now?

– I'm interested in a lot of things, unlike you.

– Game over guys. We are together to have fun. Ready to pub crawl? I
know one trendy not far on the platform. And after we have a party in an
undisclosed location.
Meryl starts getting excited.

  – Let's go to a rhythmic and drinking party!
Outside, the air doesn't turn cold. It's the heatwave. Ahead, Meryl walks
like a duck with her dancing shoes.

She starts a conversation with Albertine.

– What's your name?

– Call me Jocelyn Brown, she says with an uncurled hair scaffold.

– You sing?

– Even better. I got an eye on an international career.

– I like your sense of humor. You are particular, girl, you rock!

On the dance floor, men are crowding. They try to reward Whitney Houston, a drag queen, by giving him bills. Among these men, Tasneem dances, strutting her body in front of male, mincing around even if in this club, nobody pays attention. Most of the men are sipping what most experts would agree is the world's finest mango margarita. Albertine suddenly suffers from a stomachache.

– Sorry guys, but the gastric juices are eating up my stomach. I feel as though a wild beast is gnawing at my belly. The toilets call me...

– How lovely... mumbles Meryl with a straw between cutting teeth.

– What's the matter with Tasneem? Why did she bring us in such place? Jérôme asks to Xavier.

– She is just toying with us, watching us, seeing how we'd react.

– What is the problem? She knows that we'd never join her on the dance floor among all these men!

– She draws attention to herself, makes herself desirable and opens doors by being provocative. And in the same time she knows how to stay off the grid. It's a trap.

– I'm going in anyway!

– Very well, but at your own risk. She will drive you the wall, sure!

Jérôme joins the other men and he's already pushed over by a couple of two young latinos absorbed by the show. Finally he gets close to Tasneem while she heads to the drag queen. Her sex appeal is so strong that she doesn't need fib to get round him. Jérôme follows her in a clumsy manner while Tasneem gets around.

So Jérôme is the closest guy and the drag queen seizes his hand dancing the slow dance. The crowd goes into transe, getting over-excited. Tasneem bursts out laughing and applauds. Jérôme, getting humiliated, comes back towards the counter, head down. Albertine, Xavier and Meryl roar.

– Congratulations Tasneem, I loudly applaud that!

– Unlike you, he is brave, like a cow-boy should be, murmursTasneem to Xavier.

This confession, it's scaring the crap out of him. For the first time, a girl seems to be more interested in the shy boy than him. Even worse, this girl is gorgeous. Tasneem goes out. Xavier and Jérôme follow behind. On the boat bridge, Tasneem kisses Jérôme on the cheek whereas she flashes that bad look at his mate.

Whereupon she leaves without uttering a word, double-locking the door.

Her eyes are blank, her eyelids drooping, and her mouth perfectly-drawn in crimson. She takes a breath of the cold air and tries to focus on something.

There is a ray of sunshine and she turns slightly. She looks vague. Adele takes a deep breath and closes her eyes.

Sitting on the residence steps, she puts out her cigarette with her index finger and readjusts her floral dress. She goes to the door, enters and closes the door behind her.

Brownout. Ain't no one gonna greet him. The apartment is left with a great void. It smells a bit it's been closed up for a while. It may lead to worst-case scenario as damp patches are everywhere in the bathroom.

There is no living soul here for sure. Xavier lights the torch with his phone and heads to the room. Inside, just as he suspected, a paper is disposed on the bedside table. Xavier recognizes Adele's handwriting.

Xavier,

It has been difficult to relieve certain tough times in my life. I took a step back, I looked at the situation and I went through all the different scenarios. I came back to that moment that I wish I had taking a break. All of us go through tough time in our lives, we all make mistakes and I started thinking about how to pick yourself up and look to the next chapter in your life. My life's been turning upside down for quite a while. Maybe it's this life that you don't like anymore, or this routine that is eating away at you

inside. See the way you're acting like you're somebody else getting me frustrated. It seems that your two sides are constantly battling each other. You chose another life in which I'm not considered part of, and hence your wish is granted. You see, it's not a lot of girls turning on that got the right mind. I had nothing but time to figure out why I made certain choices and, most importantly, what do I want. And I surrounded myself with people who didn't look after my best interests. I need someone that could stand me, that be true to me. And I want to make that negative situation a positive. You crossed the line. There is no going back now. You get caught in a lie, it's sayonara, sweetheart.
Adele.

With a scornful smile, he crumples it up and drops it.

It's entirely dark in there. Jérôme bangs into the table and a bottle of wine breaks apart on the parquet.
Finally he turns on the light. He finds Xavier stood beneath the window, with tears in his eyes, an extreme violence that has been rising from him. He looks up at his ex brother-in-law, bloodshot eyes.
  – What did you expect? Pull yourself up!
Xavier doesn't answer. However he keeps looking him in the face. Jérôme goes on.
– How could she just stand there and not say anything? How can you imagine that?
– What did you tell her?
– Absolutely nothing. She got there all on her own. Don't be conceited, you have no one to blame but yourself for what you have done to my sister. But I ain't mad at cha.
  – I don't understand, went so well last time...
  – Write her.
  – What's the point? She helped me keep it real. If I could turn back the hands of time...

9

Getting of wisdom.

– Sandra, Svetlana, Junko, Kimberley...there are only girls among his friends. Do you think he accepts boys?

– Check the references. There may be some men in.

– Yes! There is one!

– Where did you get it? No, are you blind? It's a girl with short hair!

– Ok, I friend-request him. It's sink or swim.

– Wait! One of the comments that come up often is this one. Read Claire's comment.

> *Protogene is a very welcoming person. He put us in a hot-air balloon with one of his friends. It's reasonably priced.*

– There is another comment that recurs frequently.

> *Protogene can arrange for a hot air balloon tour. The price, that is the snag.*

– This is not *Couchsurfing* spirit, he blackmails us...

– Certainly, but in the same time you can use it to live an incredible experience. It's better than the hostel.

– So, what do we do?

– Send a request.

– Wait. I see a young guy who seems to be open-minded. He gets more than 100 references. The problem is, there are so many surfers that you might be sleeping on the ground.

– Pack your bag, it's open door!

– Three nights on the ground could be hard.

– We don't have the choice. Send a request, please.

– Check this profile.

I just rented a small shoebox apartment downtown. You can share the king size bed with me. But don't worry, I promise I'll stay on my side of the bed!

– How many references does he get?
– 90. All positives.
– Send a request.
– Shall we toss for it?

At the entrance to the estuary, the Nyali bridge linking the hustle and bustle of the bazaars to the business district affords splendid views of the coastal beaches. The narrow streets give access to the downtown by proceeding up toward a hill. At the top of the rise, Protogene is waiting for his guests. Three men are standing;
a svelte and fresh-faced one with a very confident stride contrasts with a little fat one with rolling gait and a kind of...waxy. Another guy, a tall fellow with those deep-set eyes, seems absent, as though asleep. He turned crimson perhaps because of the burning sun, and he fails to express himself well. By comparison, the svelte one expresses himself fluently.
  – I'm Protogene. This is Solomon and John.
With a rushed gesture, Hakan holds out his hand to Xavier and puts his hand over his heart, repeating the same with Jérôme.
  – I suggest that we go shopping, empty fridge...

The supermarket trolley is packed.
  – Here, it's halal certificate, is it good for you? asks Protogene.
When it's time to pay at the cash-desk, Protogene, assisted by Solomon and John empties everything of its contents. Xavier starts fidgeting and seeks the gaze of Jérôme. He whispers:
– Do we have to pay?
– It's, uh, it's tricky. He bought foods for one week at least and we stay just three days so...
– Protogene, I figure we could go halfsies?

– Take it easy, you're my special guests. When I come to Paris, you'll welcome me well!

The cashier stares at them:

– Frenchies?

– I tell ya... real gentlemen.

People around laugh out loud.

Outside, Protogene packs the car. Everybody get on.

> – We don't go home, we go to my cousin's, says Protogene, staring at the mirror.

The Fiat hardly survives on the bumpy country roads.

All around are echoing the sounds of spoons and teapots banging plates and cups, glasses clinking. Under a blazing summer sun, families are slumbering. The smell of coffee lingers in the air. It looks like a beautiful afternoon.

–I know everyone here. This site calms me down because you take advantage of coziness while getting a suntan. None of this could be possible anywhere else.

Protogene orders for his friends because the menu is in Swahili. When the waiter arrives with a selection of cakes and teas, Protogene throws up his hands providing a few words in his dialect. Then he takes the teapot and pours the tea out, talking to Hakan who is smoking.

> – I'm not just you hookah-smoking caterpillar, share it!

Smoking the water pipe, he stares at Jérôme.

– How will you get to Naïrobi?

– We'll take a night bus.

Protogene thinks a while.

> – Be careful, the French gotcha covered. A cousin of mine could come with you. It's safer for you. I'll call him.

Protogene grabs his cell phone and strikes up a long conversation. When he hangs up, it's already time to go.

Xavier reaches into his purse and hands him a 20 but Protogene refuses.

> – It's no charge, the owner is family.

So, with those words, he stands up and goes hugging everybody.

Inside the bazaar, the shop keepers rubs shoulders with some tourists. Protogene kind of step back and lets his friends go as they please until

Xavier sets his sights on a clothing store; Tommy Hilfiger, Ralph Lauren...pull-over and coats pile up. The excitement goes down when the seller quotes the prices.

– 160...

Protogene, who does not say a word, shows up.

– I think it's time we got this straight, sit and talk face to face 'cause I have about enough, It's not hard to see. Is there a chair in here?

– No problem my friend. Could I offer you a cup of tea? A cigarette?

Thus, they face one another. Really, we can say that there is more than a friendly atmosphere. When Protogene takes the calculator.

– Ok, for this pull, I give you 8. For this one I give you 10 max.

The seller starts sweating profusely whereas behind, people from all over Europe will soon descend upon the store to trade. Protogene keeps on bargaining.

– 50 for these two coats and 15 for the sweater. So finally I give you...wait...78. Ok?

– My friend, I feel like you want to kill me. It is quality, not made in China. Look at them, they earn their living!

– 78.

– As it's fate, I'll let you have it for. I would, but...but these coats are cashmere!

– Kidding aside, drive prices down or if you ain't running game we leave.

– My friend, these are the lowest prices. You know how much it costs me? I'm paying out more than your price. No trader, anywhere will sell something if prices are too low.

– Rouya, I saw lower prices just at the previous store! Don't rip me off.

On the verge of hysterics, the seller continues to deal. He looks at the French.

   – It is not my intention but without profit margin how am I supposed to pay my bills? Sarkozy, please, don't kill me my friends.

Protogene cuts him off.

– It's the crisis in France too, don't you know that? Make back the gains that have been lost by ripping the Germans off over there.

– I won't go on with the case...

– I don't want to fool around with you but my friends bought a lot of garments. So if that is unsatisfactory and if we can't find a way of getting it for cheaper then I suggest to my friends we go elsewhere. I don't like to be conned.

A colleague seeing the seller upset comes to help.

– Ok we stop auctions. We find an agreement on its price. What about 100?

– 78...

– Fine, stop the carnage...ok I let you have it for 78.

They shake the hands and leave, but at this moment, the seller comes back.

  – Uh, look, I can ask you a favor? Don't be stingy, give me 1 for the tea and 1 for the cigarette, please.

That day, seen from the sky, all these people walking along the highway reminds of worker ants. The night here in the bustling streets, big cats have replaced pigeons, the mullana callings are interspersed with another, echoing with the palms of the drebkis that strike drabdukas at tremendous pace. Some musicians hold their instruments under the arm while those sitting get their instrument stuck between the knees, playing flexibly. Protogene shouts at Jérôme when a shoeshine boy knocks his scrubbing brush over the ground.

  – He did it on purpose. If you pick it up he gonna offer you the service, then he claims his due.

The boy makes a face and goes.

– Guys, I have to go to the restaurant where I work now. You can visit me. How's that sound?

– Ok!

The restaurant is mostly frequented by French. Protogene puts his friends in the first table. Dressed in an apron and a chef's hat, he runs around the demanding clients.

– I go get the menu. Be comfortable, you're so uptight!

  – It's fancy. Xavier, how much is this gonna cost? whispers Jérôme.

– I suppose it's costing the earth?

Protogene comes back faster than expected. He carries a notebook and a pencil, miming writing something on, doing this for a lark.

– May I suggest you cumin balls, eggplants and aubergines with yoghurt. We can add some cheese patties. For a starter, will it do?

Xavier and Jérôme don't say anything. He barely got the time to open the mouth when Xavier catches him up.

– We would have eaten in a four stars hotel, we would be better off.

– But what would you know about Turkey if you travel alone? Take it easy.

– How many Turkish pounds you get with 1 Euro?

– Shut up, he's coming...

Protogene puts the plates on the table and takes the top off a beer bottle.

– I bring you other local beverages.

Eyes wide open, the clients in the next table watch the show. One of them smiles:

– You haven't eaten all day?

Xavier cuts into his first plate when Protogene arrives, carrying a big tray.

– Pilau bulgur from Anatolia. Bon appétit messieurs. Would you like some fizzy drinks?

The mouth full, Jérôme's head nodding no. Shortly afterwards, here he is again with a cheeseboard.

– For the dessert, I cooked chocolate mousse and Baklavas. I bring you other sodas to digest.

At this time the restaurant is empty.

– Ah, my belly's full, I feel bad, says Xavier slumping into the sofa.

Protogene is occupied in giving orders to his subordinate. He waves Xavier over to pay.

– The moment of truth comes, here comes the pain...

Protogene stabs away at the keyboard and shows the till receipt as long as your arm.

– This is your due.

Xavier reads it three times.

– Nothing to pay?

– You are my guests and anyway, the boss is not here. He's not even gonna see it, what a smuck. Also, I have eighty meals not taken.

John stays focus on the road. Exceeding the speed limit, he stays scheduled just after a local car.

– This way we are not too much, you know, like high beams and low beams.

The whole rest of the drive remains silent. John goes to the duty free center which is located just before the check point.

– I have to renew my green card.

– What is it?

– Automotive insurance is valid up to three months.

The police officer comes to talk to the driver. And after the conversation, John turns towards Xavier.

– The card costs 35 Euros. Pay cash.

– Why does he say that?

– I don't have any idea. You have the cash? Jérôme asks.

John looks at the mirror.

– Sorry but I spent all my cash down to the last coin in my pocket. Pump price is expensive... It's a toss-up whether oil prices will go up or down over the days ahead.

Xavier carries out and the policeman smiles at John who revs the engine drives off at full speed swift like the wind... and he stares at the French.

– So I hear that you were not willing to ride on a balloon? The pigeon valley it's worth seeing!

– We can't afford it. That is not provided for in our budget. 250 it's all we have.

– You're penniless, right?

John stares straight and speeds up at 80 miles an hour until Konya city where he parks the car in front of a huge highway median.

– Unfortunately, Protogene has things to do. Don't take this wrong but at the moment business is slow...Au revoir.

And the driver pushes down on the gas igniting a cloud of dust spraying to their faces.

With perplexity, the receptionist scrutinizes Xavier observing with a blank stare a bus station boycotted by tourists.

– We want two tickets for Naïrobi.

– Do you have an address?

– Not quite, or hardly what you might all an address. We stay with a friend.

– If it's a friend you should know the address, insists the receptionist, growing impatient.

– He's coming to pick us up here.

– How do you know him?

– On a website. We sent a request and he accepted.

– Which website?

– *Couchsurfing.*

– Hey Daniel, you know Cochsurfi?

The colleague much sunburned, short-legged, give them an amused look.

– Couchesurfi? I don't know but that looks good. Couchesurfi...with ketchup or mayonnaise?

Everybody laugh like seals, fostering the dialogue. Beads of sweat begin to appear on Xavier's forehead. The receptionist carries on cross-questioning the unusual suspect.

– How do you move throughout the country?

– Night bus, answers Jérôme.

– Hey Paul, they might have just as easily slit their throat!

The seals restart laughing in chorus.

– It's a joke, don't be afraid, our country is safe and everybody is kind!

After giving himself time to think, the receptionist takes a peek at them, stamps and adds:

– Enjoy your stay.

– Two armed guards come closest. They eye each other suspiciously belch away in the silence.

– Well, first of all, wipe that suspicious look off your face. The guard with facial injuries goes up to Xavier and yell at him, spitting in his face.

– You're in a zone forbidden to civilians like you! he says in a commanding tone.

Xavier presents his passport. The guard takes it and scrutinizes it like a teacher scrutinizes a test sheet.

– Let's go to the custody!

Xavier operates. Jérôme follows but the other guard pushes him back with the rifle stock.

– Stay out! Wait here till my superior checks your stuff.

Inside the office, a fat commander slumped in his chair in front of the screen and... at first, Xavier thinks he'd just fallen asleep. The fat man stares at him.

– It's 500 dollars sir.

– What?

– Don't play coy with me. You walked in a forbidden field. Are you a spy? Your friend can leave but you, you stay with us.

Xavier starts to sweat. He thinks for a few moments.

– Ok. I call the French Ambassy.

– Why?

– I would like to hear whether this is actually a legal procedure.

– The commander hardly stands up. He's motioning the guard to let it down.

– My friend, let's not have that discussion all over again. Everything is fine. Kagiso ! Kagiso !

The guard that stayed out get in.

– Kagiso ! Bring us the Mnazi! Hurry up!

Jérôme sits next to Xavier.

– Mnazi, you know that?

– Is it fish? asks Jérôme.

– Tchié ! Freakin' banana benders. It's a wine! We produce it with palm trees!

They swig the bottle together.

Jérôme and Xavier had been forced to hitchhike to join Naïrobi. The driver doesn't speak any English word. Outside, the ground has signs of ageing. Gusty winds reduce visibility. The twisty roads alongside a peaceful village is covered by a red dust and the way is delayed by crumbling roadsides. It seems to them that they are stuck in a rut every 1 km. It's not what you might call a well-traveled road, and most of the time you can see some cartages passing through the village. An old man on horseback, from the top of his saddle, looks at them up and down. The driver explains the deal and the reaction of the man proves that he understood. He proposes to show the way to reach the house of Sauveur. A red smoke from the skyline comes to the three men, soon soothed by an enhancing, calming, warm, earthy summer breeze that shifts to the north-east.

A dust-drenched extends across the shallow valley until it reaches the minaret of the main mosque. The way to the nearby village offers a row of whitewhashed houses. Some arabesques run along the façades. In front of the door, eight pairs of sneakers smashed on the floor. On the doorstep, an old man stands with difficulty. He is the same as a pile of bones that supports a skin sort of hanging off. He hunkers down and looks at the strangers. After a few seconds he turns around.

– Osman, someone is there.

The old man slips away. A wiry guy stands behind. Who would not have slit eyes? He got so much slanted-eyes that it seem a fold among others skin folds. His arches are hairless, the skin is tanned, a generous smile.

– Who are you?

Jérôme is taken aback, Xavier seems to be in a daze. The guy weren't expecting them.

   – I'm Jérôme, and he's Xavier... you are Osman or Sauveur?

The guy looks kinda cool. He smiles.

– My name is Osman, but please call me Sauveur. One day, an American guy had a rough time in the company of a couchsurfer. Following that, I proposed him to couch here during two weeks. He was so grateful that he decided to give me this name. I like that.

Inside, the ground is covered by poor quality carpets that we use to find in a refuge. On the sofa, several young guys are chatting. They introduce themselves, each in turn; Imran from Pakistan, Davut from Turkey, Kwan from South Korea, Helina and Kermo, a couple from Estonia, Karolina from Sweden and thereby Sauveur's girlfriend. This one gets the floor.

– You are the French? Welcome!

– Thank you. You live here? questions Xavier.

– I've lived here two years already.

– She came as a surfer and never left, cuts off Sauveur.

This kind of revelation never fails to get a big laugh. At this moment, the Korean guy is taping away at his computer.

– What are you doing? asks Sauveur.

– I send an alert to the administrator to ban a French boy who is more than rude.

– What is he doing?

– He's constantly threatening the web surfers to bury them in his yard. And he's barely 16...

Sauveur turns towards Xavier.

– What do you say if we have tea outside the house?

Around a table, all the young have private conversation. Jérôme speaks to Kwan.

– You done a lot of *Couchsurfing*?

– For a year yes. I was in Istanbul the week before. Last month I surfed in New-York. I've been very lucky because this city is the most popular. New-York receives the most requests of the world. Only one person accepted me over more than hundred requests sent!

Jérôme looks at Sauveur.

– How do you manage to host so many people?

– Each surfer is unique and deserves to be welcomed. It is fair to say that there's not much room,we'd be a bit intimate. Not easy, but we're making it work. With some pillows everybody is able to sleep on the floor.

– For me it's the sofa, smiles Kwan.

– You arrived last so, would you mind if you take the floor?

– I don't care, confesses Jérôme.

Another surfer sits down. He's from Malaysia.

– I forgot him. Actually we are ten tonight.

– It's everyday the same?

– More or less, cuts off Karolina. Sometimes we take a short break.

Sauveur tells off:

– I get fucking cut off! I'm really pissed off! I wasn't finished with the story! Besides, finish the dishes I've prepared!

A true staging aimed at the surfers is taking place. A staging in which the couple loves to rehearse to the amusement of the visitors as soon as there is an opportunity to do so. A sort of pleasure. Karolina, freezing to death, wraps herself in a blanket.

– But Osman, I've got a fever...

– Karolina, please, don't upset me and eat!

She stares at him with blinking of eyelids.

– So I don't sleep on your side, I'm going to contaminate you...

Hearing that, Kwan gets anxious.

– So you sleep on couch tonight?

– Don't worry Kwan, we must lie back to back, so keep the couch, says Sauveur.

Then he speaks to Jérôme.

– What happened? You said you'd be coming from Istanbul in two days.

– Our host insisted that we go around in a balloon... when we turn him down, he used business as an excuse to throw us out.

– He's not a couchsurfer. He got an enterprising mind. Quite a number of people act like this.

Sauveur looks away.

– Well, I'm putting together a last-minute meeting. Usually we gather with all the surfers once a week. My friend Polycarpe is waiting for us...

– No problem, we come with you.

Around the bend, the Jeep stops down the grand Villa. It looks like some sort of bunker. Karolina calls Polycarpe.

– Hey, here we are!

– Come in!

The heavy doors open. Everyone hop off except Karolina who steps on the pedal.

Inside the villa, Polycarpe is getting high up on the balcony. He's wearing a rumpled shirt.

– Where is Karolina?

– I think she went to the store, says Kwan.

– Yeah, that's not gonna do it. It's embarrassing when she does... Wait, I'll go down with you. I just want to sit by the pool and drink Pina Coladas all day.

All the surfers are seated round the couches. The Estonians are traveling light, likely on foot. He is unemployed and she took a year off.

– We couchsurf most of the time and we hitchhike. It's really easy in the area, she says.

– So all you guys are staying with Osman? That's cool.

– Yep, it's a bit squished there, laughs Kwan.

– You surprise me! I asked Karolina if she wanted to meet for a drink and have plenty of time together, taking some time off, getting a tan, chilling... I got five rooms. I own my own Marijuana farm in one of them. By the way, Karolina declined! She's not too high on the idea! Ok, did you face with bad experiences on Couchsurfing, tell me?

– Not really, confesses Jérôme. We have had some wonderful times. And we went through some bad time once.

– What kind?

– In Spain. A tactile animal. He touched us everytime. And he broadcasted a porn movie.

– No, that's crazy! But you ran off?

– The next day.

– You'd better to comb through profiles. It's sex-surfing! Hein, Karolina may not show it yet ! She's got some crazy plan she's come up with and you're playing right into it and I'm not.

– Some host can declined at the last minute, says Kwan.

– Badmouth him to everybody you know!

– Yeah, but the guy probably deletes his profile and creates another one shortly after.

– Ok, we take a swim?

It's dark already and Osman never showep up. Polycarpe drives the group home. He phones to Karolina.

– My dear, your friends are amazing! I love Couchsurfing, I really need to sign up and pick a group like this!

It's been nearly two hours now since Jérôme stares at the ceiling. It's 7:03. The coach for Kigali is leaving at 9:00. He wakes up. Everyone around is snoring.

– Xavier, I know it's extremely cruel to awaken you at such an hour. But we have to go now. Sauveur shows up.

   – My friends, it's time to go. Maybe we can be stuck in traffic. The minibus for Kigali station will be here in 5 minutes.

By the roadside, a minibus full of people doesn't stop. The next is following, just as crowded. Jérôme is getting nervous.

   – It's 8:10.

   – Don't worry, the next one is for us.

It's 8:17, a minibus is coming. Sauveur asks the passengers to make room. They have to pile in the vehicle and they crawl their way back in.

Jérôme is checking his watch.

– Driver, branch off or let us down.

Sauveur barely puts feet on the ground that already three boda bodas slam the break.

– Musungus ! they yell.

– Musungus means the white man, explains Sauveur. This is the only chance we've got of finding the coach for Kigali.

Each one of them saddled their motorcycles and threw on their helmets. Sauveur took one of Jérôme's two bags. The three boda bodas .... Across the more and more chaotic traffic. No one looked twice as motorcycles crossed between sidewalk and street through the stalls of textile merchants and shoppers. Saveur's driver suddenly stopped at the roundabout, hesitating briefly before taking a sharp right, losing trace of those pursuing.

Epilogue.

The wind rises, raising the red ochre dust all around. Jérôme and Xavier are walking, more or less. A boy is on their way. His face is barely visible. He belongs to one of the nine tribes, the kikuyu tribe.
-Musungus, have you seen a young girl? She's white with blond hair. She's German. I was his guide for two days in Mombasa. I've been looking for her for weeks.
First, they think it's a joke. So they don't react as quickly.
- Sorry, we don't...
- She was traveling by Couchsurfing. She was so kind and she'd put blind trust in me. I miss her.
-Really?
- Yes. She was looking for a guide. She was traveling alone. She needed me around her all the time in the bazaars, market places, temple. At one point, she decided to buy a souvenir. I was in charge of the deal with the seller. She gave me her wallet and stayed out. It was feeling like something was there. She put, like, 6 bucks in there. I could have run away. But guess what? Nothing happened. The last night we slept in the desert. She let me kiss her, once... In reality, she was freezing cold and she wanted someone round her. Of course she accepted me to sleep aside but here was the deal: sleeping backs turned, feet there, head there. Otherwise the deal was off!
-That story sounds crazy!
-I love her... I'm desperate. I've looked everywhere. That's why I came to Nairobi. I took the bus last night. There's no future for me out there. I want to go to Germany to find her.
Against all odds, a girl appears when he turns around.
-I can't believe it...

At the overcrowded airport, Jérôme rushes towards the departure lounge for Mexico. Behind, Xavier and Albertine are exchanging greetings despite the emergency. Xavier is grumbling.
– You've got nothing better to do that come with us?
– Nothing better!

– And what about Rwanda? You intend to go? Hold on, keep an eye on my suitcase, I need to go to the toilets.
– Your suitcase? You can have it!
While Albertine follows Jérôme, Xavier leaves for a moment.
– Jérôme, can we trade places? There can be no question of sitting next to Xavier!
Jérôme checks on his phone that nobody changes plans. After Bogota, the way will continue to Medellin and Bucaramanga where Ana lives. During the flight, faces that pass through the rearview; Dzana the Bosnian, Ana the Colombian, Jin-Sang the Korean, Zlatko the Croatian, Iga the Portuguese, Walter the American, Ann-Josie and Jean-Benoit the Quebecker, Sauveur the Kenyan... He hopes to remember them evermore.

He wakes up in a cold sweat. Xavier's face sinks into his thinking. Jérôme drags himself to the closet. When he is dressed in his uniform he looks at himself in the mirror and sees his stressed face for several minutes before slamming the door.

He lets the vacuum of space smother it. He keeps his eyes outside failing to notice the coffee drips down on his Carlington. Today, it's been ten months since he starts working in European Union Department. His former colleagues start their summer holidays.
   – Jérôme, they are expecting us at the meeting room.
The voice of Mr Dilan, his immediate superior, hammers in his head like a pinball. Jérôme throws the drink and takes out a handkerchief to clean up the shoe. The Minister arrives at top speed from the end of the corridor, escorted by his councilors, and he nods his head to Jérôme who slows the pace down as he gets closer to the room. The question he's getting to is, does he have the courage to grab the dream that picked him, that befit him and grips him; or will he let it get away and slip through? Jérôme saunters over the corridor. Now he seems not to control the body language that he has been mastering since he's little, like...erased from his cells. However, just passing room, with long strides, his feet gradually come off the ground. Now he got his knees high, inexorably glued to the exit, never looking back, a smile coming to his face.

www.ingramcontent.com/pod-product-compliance
Lightning Source LLC
LaVergne TN
LVHW010645200726
843507LV00011B/1764